TAKING THE WAR TO SANTA ANNA

Pandemonium reigned both outside and within Santa Anna's quarters. The protection offered by the striped walls of the tent might be inadequate, but at least it served to keep those inside concealed from the archer in the darkness.

As he saw the first of the sentries run around the end of the marquee, Tommy reached for another arrow. By the time he had completed his draw and aim, the sentry was close enough to be able to see him. Skidding to a halt, the soldier started to raise his carbine.

Forward darted the Oriental's arrow. It took the Dragoon in the right breast before he could raise his weapon. A scream of agony burst from him as he twirled helplessly around. The carbine slipped from his hands, and they clutched spasmodically at the feathered remnant of the missile, which was all he could reach. Sprawling to the ground, he lay shrieking and writhing in torment for a few seconds before becoming limp and motionless.

•

Ole Devil
at San Jacinto

J. T. EDSON

A DELL BOOK

Published by
Dell Publishing
a division of
Bantam Doubleday Dell Publishing Group, Inc.
666 Fifth Avenue
New York, New York 10103

ISBN: 0-440-21040-2

Printed in the United States of America

Published simultaneously in Canada

January 1992

10 9 8 7 6 5 4 3 2 1

OPM

IN EXPLANATION

Realizing that there was no hope of obtaining a satisfactory—or even a peaceful—settlement of their differences with the Mexican government,[1] particularly after *Presidente* Antonio Lopez de Santa Anna had consolidated his position as absolute dictatorial ruler, the colonists in the Territory of the State of Coahuila, known as Texas,[2] had accepted that they must be prepared for an all-out war. Even before any attempt had been made to set up a formally constituted Republic of Texas, Samuel Houston had been given the rank of major general and instructed to organize an army. At the same time prominent

1. New readers can find in the author's *Young Ole Devil* a detailed account of why the Anglo-U.S.-born colonists, who called themselves Texians (the *i* would be dropped from usage after annexation by the United States of America and the subsequent Mexican War of 1846–48), as well as many of the Mexican-born Chicano citizens of Texas, decided to break away from Mexico's domination.—*J.T.E.*

2. One of the major contributory factors was the Mexican authorities' continued refusal to make Texas a separate state with full representation in the government. To the Texians this was similar to the "no taxation without representation" issue, which had caused the break with Great Britain in 1776 and the foundation of the United States of America.—J.T.E.

and wealthy Texians, such as James Bowie, William Barrett
Travis, Edward Burleson, Benjamin Milam, James Walker Fannin, Frank Johnson, and the Hardin, Fog, and Blaze clan, dom-
iciled on their vast land grant along the Rio Hondo, had raised
regiments—few of which had a strength exceeding a couple of
hundred men—ready for the bloody fray they all knew was
forthcoming.

The earlier stages of the rebellion, during the last months of
1835, had been successful as far as the colonists' efforts were
concerned. Several minor skirmishes had gone in their favor, as
had their only major confrontation with the Mexican Army.
On December 11, following the battle which had lasted for six
days,[3] *el Presidente*'s brother-in-law, General Martin Perfecto
de Cós and his force of eleven hundred men had surrendered to
Colonel Burleson at San Antonio de Bexar. In spite of objections from several of his subordinate officers, Burleson had allowed all of their prisoners to return unharmed to Mexico upon
his having received Cós's word that he and the released men
would refrain from any further hostile action against the Texians and Chicanos.

The protests against accepting the promise had proved to be
justifiable.

Early in 1836, satisfied that he had established himself in
complete control of all Mexican territory south of the Rio
Bravo—which the Texians were already calling the Rio Grande
—Santa Anna marched north with the avowed intention of
crushing the rebellion and driving the "foreign land thieves"
from Texas. With this column, blatantly disregarding the
pledge he had given at San Antonio de Bexar, was General Cós.

While the earlier successes had boosted the morale of the
Republic of Texas's all too small army, they had proved a
mixed blessing in that they had presented a false impression of
the struggle that lay ahead. As Houston and other farsighted
Texians had appreciated, their victories had been gained against
poorly armed, badly trained, and ineffectively commanded

3. One of the Texians' casualties was Colonel Benjamin Milam, killed by a
sniper during the street and house-to-house fighting.—J.T.E.

troops. Due to the fact that Texas was so far from the center of Mexican affairs, thereby offering few chances of distinction or promotion, career officers of good quality were disinclined to serve there.

Such men were marching north with Santa Anna. They were leading battle-hardened veterans, soldiers who had fought almost continuously in the various interfactional struggles that had plagued their country ever since it had wrested independence from Spain in 1824. As Houston knew, they would prove a more dangerous proposition than anything so far faced by the Texians, particularly because they would have a tremendous advantage in numbers.

Having accepted that war with Mexico was inevitable and unavoidable, as well as realizing that aid would be needed if victory was to be obtained, a commission, headed by Stephen Fuller Austin, had been dispatched to the United States of America. They had a dual purpose: to obtain a supply of arms and ammunition and also to sound out the possibility of having their republic annexed to become a part of that country. Many of the colonists, Houston and the Hardin, Fog, and Blaze clan being prominent in their number, believed that attaining statehood offered their only hope for a safe and prosperous future.

The first objective of the commission, handled by Marsden Fog, had been successful. A number of volunteers had been persuaded to go to Texas and help in the struggle. Supporters had also procured a consignment of five hundred new caplock rifles, each with a bayonet, and a large quantity of ammunition. For diplomatic reasons these had been delivered secretly, and the army had not as yet taken charge of them.[4]

The commission's second purpose was achieving less decisive results. There was no unanimity of opinion on the matter of annexation in the United States. While many people saw the potential benefit of acquiring such a large area of developable land, others disagreed. Nor had the commission's suggestion achieved the desired agreement—that, because of the enormous

4. How the consignment was delivered and transported is told in *Ole Devil and the Caplocks* and *Ole Devil and the Mule Train.*—J.T.E.

territory involved, Texas could be subdivided into three or four
separate states. The very vocal antislavery faction opposed the
idea on the grounds that to accept might lead to the creation of
more so-called slave states. They had tried to influence public
opinion further by pointing out that a great many criminals had
"gone to Texas"[5] and that all the colonists were tarred with the
same illegal brush.

Being all too aware of the disparity in numbers between the
force under his command and the army that Santa Anna would
be able to put into the field, Houston had not waited to find out
the results of the commission's endeavors. He had appreciated
the folly of attempting to meet such overwhelmingly superior
strength in open battle except under his own terms and upon
ground of *his* choosing. With that in mind, on learning the
Mexicans were approaching the Rio Grande, he had ordered a
withdrawal of all colonists into East Texas. Once there, he had
announced, they could select the most advantageous point at
which to make a stand, and if things should go badly, the survi-
vors would have an avenue of escape by crossing the border
into the United States.

In addition to carrying out the withdrawal, the general had
wanted to adopt what would one day become known as a
scorched-earth policy. By destroying their abandoned homes,
standing crops, and everything else they could neither drive nor
carry away, the colonists would have left their pursuers with a
supply problem that would have grown increasingly difficult as
Santa Anna advanced further into Texas. Despite having had
the reasons for such drastic behavior explained to them, there
had been most strenuous objections to the idea. When Houston
had caused the town of Gonzales to be put to the torch, the
assembled Texians and Chicanos had come so close to mutiny

5. *Gone to Texas* meant to be at odds with the law in the United States.
Many wanted men entered Texas during the colonization period and would
continue to do so until annexation on February 16, 1846. Until the latter
became a fact, they had known there was little danger of being arrested and
extradited by the local authorities.—J.T.E.

that he was compelled to refrain from continuing the destruction along his line of march.

Nor was the refusal to adopt what would have been a sound tactic—particularly as Santa Anna was to burn the deserted properties after looting them—the only problem facing the general. Many of the Texians and Chicanos, especially the latter, who were faced with the prospect of having to give up their homes, realized that *el Presidente* would show no mercy to any of them who fell into his clutches. For all that, there had not been a unanimous acceptance of the necessity to withdraw. In fact, with disastrous results in each case, three separate parties had elected to do otherwise.

Even before the withdrawal had been begun, Colonel Frank Johnson, wishing to gain acclaim and to loot, had begun to gather a force with the intention of—as he put it—carrying the war to the enemy by invading Mexico along the Coast Road. To this end he had even gone so far as to attempt to seduce members of Houston's main body from their duty. He had been thwarted in this and was still trying to raise sufficient support when the Tamaulipa Brigade, under the command of General José Urrea, had swept northward. Attacking unexpectedly on February 26, Urrea had taken Johnson's party by surprise at the town of San Patricio and routed them. Although their casualties had been only sixteen killed and twenty-one taken prisoner (they were later executed), the remainder scattered and fled. Johnson himself escaped.

An even more tragic fate had befallen the second group, but at least their purpose was honorable and potentially beneficial to the colonists' cause. Under the joint command of colonels William Barrett Travis, James Bowie—after whom the all-purpose, basic fighting knife that he had made famous was named [6] —and the recently arrived David "Davey" Crockett, one hundred and eighty-three men had volunteered to remain at the old

6. What happened to James Bowie's knife after his death during the final onslaught upon the Alamo Mission is told in *The Quest for Bowie's Blade*. New readers can find information about the "bowie" type of knife in Appendix A.—J.T.E.

Franciscan Order's Mission San Antonio de Valera. Built with
the qualities of a fort as much as of a place of worship, it was
more commonly referred to as the Alamo Mission on account
of it once having been surrounded by a grove of *alamo* plains
cottonwood, *Populus sargentii,* trees. Their assignment was to
hold on for as long as possible, delaying Santa Anna's main
force while their comrades-in-arms were retiring to the east. In
addition they hoped to gain time in which Houston could as-
semble the whole of the Republic of Texas's scattered forces.
When these were gathered and, possibly, reinforced with volunteers from the United States, the general could make ready for
the final confrontation. They had accepted that by carrying out
their commitment they might not escape with their lives, and
they intended to make their deaths as costly as possible for *el
Presidente.*

Conceding that the stand at the Alamo Mission would be
helpful to his strategy, Houston had agreed to it. He had also
offered to send in more men, who might even turn the tide in
the Texians' favor.

For thirteen days, until the final mass assault on March 6,
1836, the band of greatly outnumbered defenders continued to
hold the Alamo Mission. Nor were they deterred by the fact
that, through no fault of their commanding general, the promised reinforcements failed to arrive. At last, inevitably, Santa
Anna's force had breached the walls. Once inside they had
carried out his threat that no quarter would be given. It was
believed that every male survivor of the bitter and bloody fighting had been slaughtered.[7] Yet, in dying, the gallant little party
had gone far toward doing what they had intended. They had
inflicted so many casualties upon their assailants during the
siege that one very senior Mexican officer was said to have
announced at the conclusion of the fighting, "Another 'victory'
like this will defeat us."

---

7. Recent research suggests that one male defender, a Chicano, José Maria
"Brigido" Guerrero, survived the massacre at the Alamo Mission by persuading his captors that he was a loyal Mexican who had been taken prisoner and held against his will by the garrison all through the siege.—J.T.E.

No such noble ideals, nor any useful motives, had been responsible for the fate of the third and by far largest group of dissidents.

Under the ineffectual command of Colonel James Walker Fannin, over four hundred of the colonists' best armed and best equipped men had been stationed in the grandiloquently named Fort Defiance at Goliad. Having failed to supply the promised reinforcements for the defenders of the Alamo Mission, using Johnson's defeat at San Patricio as an excuse, Fannin finally attempted to carry out an order from Houston. Destroying the fort on March 9, he and his men set out to join the main body of the army.

Not far from Goliad they were surrounded by the Tamaulipa Brigade, which was moving westward in a leisurely fashion, looting and destroying property in passing. Fannin ordered his men to surrender after only a token resistance. Their lack of aggression did not produce the dividends that Fannin had hoped for. Although their captors told them that they would be free to go provided they gave their promise to quit Texas forever, they were marched from the town on Palm Sunday, March 27. Apart from a few who contrived to escape, they were massacred in cold blood.[8]

While these events—which, for the sake of convenience, have been dealt with as separate episodes—were taking place, there were other developments occurring elsewhere.

On March 2 a convention had assembled at Washington-on-the-Brazos, and Texas was formally declared to be a free and independent republic under the Lone Star flag. A provisional government was established, with Henry Smith and James W. Robinson appointed respectively governor and lieutenant governor. However, in a short while, Smith was replaced by David G. Burnet, who adopted the title president. None of these activities made any noticeable change in the conduct of the campaign. The professional politicians, in what was announced would be the republic's capital city, played no part in the military operations beyond offering advice to Houston, which

8. Told in *Get Urrea.*—J.T.E.

would have been either impossible or disastrous to put into effect.

One thing the hard-pressed general had not needed from the provisional government was the kind of advice it and its opposition was showering upon him. He had sufficient problems of his own without needing such "help." He was already having to contend with the type of men who formed the bulk of his command.

In spite of the propaganda put out by Benjamin Lundy and the antislavery faction in the United States, only a small proportion of the colonists had "gone to Texas." The majority were decent, honest, law abiding, and hardworking. However, a man had to be endowed with considerable feelings of self-sufficiency before embarking upon such a daring project as migrating with his family to the vast and hostile Texas of that period. Skilled in the use of weapons, the average colonist tended to be a rugged individualist who preferred to rely upon his own judgment. Taking orders, or accepting discipline was foreign to his nature. In general, he knew nothing of teamwork and less about strategy.

Unless one remembered these points, it was difficult to understand their forces' fiascos during the early months of 1836, considering their courage and proven fighting ability.

It said much for Houston's personality—aided by the backing of loyal supporters with the wisdom to see he was adopting the only possible tactics under the circumstances—that he had contrived to hold together so large a proportion of the army. He had needed all of his persuasive powers to have his suggestions accepted. Even so, when the main body had reached Gonzales, on the eastern bank of the Guadalupe River, he was compelled by the weight of public opinion to halt in the hope that some definite action could be taken.

Feelings had been running high among the general's force all through the days of the siege at the Alamo Mission. There were many demands for an attempt to be made to relieve their embattled comrades-in-arms. However, the evening of March 12 brought confirmation of the terrible news that the Alamo had fallen. As no help would be needed, Houston had ordered the withdrawal to be resumed. To reduce the protests, he had promised that he would consider making a stand on the Colorado River provided Fannin and the Fort Defiance contingent joined them.

With the general and his army once again retiring, the politicians did nothing to improve the situation. On March 18, in what was to become known as the Runaway Scrape, they fled from Washington-on-the-Brazos to set up what they referred to as a temporary capital at the little town of Harrisburg. Once there, they gave Houston a respite from their attentions. According to the reports he received, they were more concerned with obtaining stationery, accommodation, furniture, and other such vital necessities for the correct functioning of a government, including "liquors suitable for genteel men to drink."

Left to his own devices by the politicians, although their behavior did nothing to improve the army's morale, the general was still experiencing the gravest difficulties with the men under his command. News of Fannin's surrender arrived on March 25 and ended any hope of making a stand on the Colorado River. The general's new argument, against which not even the most irresponsible of the hotheads who were clamoring for a fight could disagree, was that the army must continue to escort the ever-growing number of refugees who were fleeing to the east. As he stated (and he was backed by Colonel Edward Fog of the Texas Light Cavalry and the aged but very capable chief of scouts, "Deaf" Smith), not until the now-homeless women and children were safely beyond the reach of Santa Anna's main force and the Tamaulipa Brigade could any confrontation be considered.

Amid all of the general's trials and tribulations, he had one thing in his favor. Having reduced the Alamo Mission, Santa Anna did not immediately continue his pursuit of the "foreign-land thieves." Instead, perhaps wishing to give his men time to forget how they had suffered over six hundred casualties—close to a third of his main force—during the thirteen days' fighting, he had spent a fortnight celebrating his "victory" in and around San Antonio de Bexar. Nor, when the pursuit was resumed, did his army show any sign of being in a hurry to catch up with their departing foes. In fact, believing that he had crushed the colonists' will to resist, *el Presidente* was considering returning to Mexico City and leaving his subordinates to drive them out of Texas.

Houston was finding that Santa Anna's lack of activity had its disadvantages as well as its blessings. Shepherding along the refugees, the Republic of Texas's Army reached San Felipe on the western shore of the Brazos River on March 31. Again yielding to the pressure from his men and encouraged by his scouts' reports regarding the behavior of their pursuers, Houston halted to reassess the situation.

It was then that the news of how Fannin and his men had been massacred by Urrea was delivered.

There was serious unrest over the tidings!

Houston knew that some action must be taken!

What follows is the story of the action decided upon by the general and how it turned out.

1

CAP'N DEVIL'S ON THE WARPATH

Captain Jackson Baines Hardin's face was like a thundercloud as he strode along the main street of San Felipe. In every direction there were signs that the Republic of Texas's small army and a large number of refugees were encamped just beyond the city limits. However, glaring straight ahead, he seemed to have eyes for nothing that was going on around him.

A few members of the Texas Light Cavalry's Company C were among the enlisted men of various regiments who were taking their ease on either side of the street. They watched with interest as their young commanding officer stalked—there was no better way of describing his mode of progression—toward them. Then, before he arrived, they began to exchange glances.

"I don't know what's riling him," commented a leathery old-timer. "But Cap'n Devil's on the warpath."

"Only thing *I* know," the youngest member of the trio went on, studying the approaching figure and sounding slightly relieved, "is that I'm sure's hell's for sinners pleased it's not *me*'s he's riled at."

"Would the captain have any reason to be after *your* hide, Stepin?" inquired the tall, well-built, blond man whose bearing was suggestive of military training and who exuded an aura of authority despite the fact that his attire bore no conventional insignia to denote that he was superior in rank to his companions.[1]

"*Me?*" the youngest soldier yelped, his voice and attitude earnestly denying the accusation. "No, sir, Sergeant, I've done learned my lesson. So I've not done a single, solitary thing wrong at all." Then he let out a sigh as the captain went by without showing the slightest awareness of the trio's presence. "Well, it looks like it isn't us he's after at all."

There was something satanic about the appearance of the young man who was the subject of the soldiers' conversation. It was that which, in part at least, had been responsible for his nickname, Ole Devil.[2]

A wide-brimmed, low-crowned black hat—of a style that had grown popular when the behavior of the successive leaders in their adopted country made the Anglo-Saxon colonists develop an ever-growing antipathy toward everything of Mexican origin, including the sombrero—hung by its *barbiquejo* chinstrap on the captain's squarely set shoulders. It left bare black hair, which was combed above his temples to convey an impression of a pair of small horns. The lines of his tanned face were enhanced by somewhat prominent cheekbones, an aquiline nose, eyebrows like inverted V's, a neatly trimmed mustache, and a short, sharp-pointed chin beard. Combined they created a Mephistophelian effect, which resembled the way artists generally depicted the physiognomy of the devil.

Just over six feet in height, twenty-five years of age, Ole Devil was slender without being puny or skinny. In fact his erect posture and swiftly striding gait were suggestive of a whipcord strength. He wore the type of uniform supplied by the Hardin, Fog, and Blaze clan for the members of their regi-

1. Although insignia was not really necessary in such a small regiment, the type of bandanna worn indicated rank in the Texas Light Cavalry. Enlisted men's were black, noncommissioned officers' green. Officers selected their own colors.—J.T.E.
2. Another reason was his reputation of being a "lil ole devil for a fight." Details of Ole Devil Hardin's background and weapons are given in Appendix A.—J.T.E.

ment[3] around his throat was knotted a tightly rolled silk ban-
dana that was a riot of brilliantly clashing colors. His fringed
buckskin shirt was tucked into tight-legged fawn riding
breeches that ended neatly in the tops of his well-polished Hessian boots.[4] A broad black belt around his waist supported an
ivory-hilted James Black bowie knife. However, for some reason, he had left off the percussion-fired Manton pistol that usually rode—butt forward so as to be accessible to either hand—
in the wide, slanting leather loop at the right.

"Seems to poor lil old me that Cap'n Devil's been more'n a
mite edgy since him, Mr. Blaze, 'n' Tommy Okasi brought back
that young lieutenant's got away when Fannin got all them
good old boys 'mass-ee-creed' by Urrea," the elderly soldier
remarked. "Which I don't blame him none at all. It's not a
thing a man likes to think on when he can't do nothing about
it."

"Huh!" Stepin sniffed, oozing truculence. "*I* can't see why
we don't just head on down Goliad way and hand Urrea his
needings."

"That's why General Sam, Colonel Fog, and Cap'n
Hardin're officers and you're not," Sergeant Smith said drily,
while the old-timer turned a sardonic gaze at the youngster.
"They've got enough sense to know we haven't enough men to
do it."

"There's been some talk about Lieutenant Dimmock saving
his skin the way he did," Stepin announced, clearly desiring to
change the subject. "Fact being, I've heard it said—"

"So have I!" Smith interrupted, turning a prohibitive frown
upon the youngster. "And, seeing's he's an officer in *our* company now, I don't want to hear it again. He got away during
the massacre, sure, but nobody with an ounce of good sense can

3. When the Hardin, Fog, and Blaze clan re-formed the Texas Light Cavalry to fight in the War of Secession (1861–65), they adopted a uniform that
conformed with the *Manual of Dress Regulations* issued by the Confederate
States' army.—J.T.E.
4. Hessian boots: Footwear originally designed for use by light cavalry such
as Hussars, having low heels, legs that extend to just below the knee, and a
V-shaped notch at the front.—J.T.E.

blame him for *that*. And, after he had, he didn't just up and keep on running like Johnson's bunch. He headed out this way to let us know what had happened, so we wouldn't sit around here just waiting for Fannin's men to join us."

"Way you're talking, Stepin-boy," the old-timer drawled, "sounds like you've been listening to some of them fancy-Dan New Orleans Wildcats's've come down this ways to teach us igner-ant Texians how to fight Santa Anna."

"They've been doing some talking," the youngster admitted, meaning to go on and disclaim any agreement with what had been said.

"Too damned much," Sergeant Smith stated coldly, his manner implying that the subject was closed.

"Looks like Cap'n Devil's headed for officers' country," the oldest soldier put in laconically. "Which, whatever it be's's riling him, it's likely not to do with us common folks, and I'm one who's content to let it stop right there." His eyes, undimmed by age, flickered to the blond noncom. "Fact being, was *somebody* to ask me if I'd take a drink in his company, I'd force myself to go ag'in' my good 'n' gawd-fearing upbringing and say, 'I'd admire to, sir.'"

"Jube," Smith answered, but he was continuing to watch his commanding officer. "Was *you-all* just once to ask us if we'd care to take a drink on *you*, we'd likely swoon clear away from the shock."

For all his levity, the sergeant was both puzzled and concerned. Since enlisting in the Texas Light Cavalry, he had grown to respect the satanic-faced young captain and, after having won promotion in the field, to know him very well. Everything about Ole Devil warned that he was angry. The signs were now indicative that the cause was to be found in the Grand Hotel. As Jube had said, the establishment had become accepted as "officers' country," and enlisted men did not patronize it.

An intelligent man, Smith took an active interest in what was going on around him. So he had heard and noticed certain things that he suspected were connected with the latter part of the conversation he had just had with his companions. He did

not care for the possibilities aroused by some of his deductions.
A loyal subordinate, he wondered if his assumptions over whatever might be taking his captain into the Grand Hotel were
correct. If they were, he hoped that Ole Devil would avoid any
actions that might bring upon him the wrath and disapproval
of his superiors.

2

I'LL DO MORE THAN JUST
PROD

Still moving as if marching in review before Major General Samuel Houston, Ole Devil Hardin passed through the main entrance of the Grand Hotel. Ignoring the clerk behind the reception desk, he went to the open door of the barroom. Crossing the threshold, he surveyed his surroundings with a sweeping glance. Although the time was only just after two o'clock in the afternoon, there were customers present. Only a few had on formal military uniforms. The attire of the remainder ranged from the coonskin caps and buckskins of lean, white-haired old "Deaf" Smith and two of his scouts at the counter, through the *vaquero* costume of a couple of Chicanos and town suits of the Texians, to the more elegant raiment worn by half a dozen young men seated around one of the tables. They were dressed in the latest style of riding clothes that had become popular among wealthy Louisianans and, in particular, among New Orleans' French-Creole dandies.

After glancing at the other occupants of the room, Ole Devil's cold-eyed scrutiny came to rest upon a young man standing —"propping himself up" would be a more apt term—against the counter and holding a schooner of beer. Matching the captain in height, he was far more bulky and lacked any evidence of a martial posture. In fact his whole bearing seemed to exude a contented lassitude. His garments were those of a member of the Texas Light Cavalry. In addition to his presence in San Felipe's best hotel, his scarlet silk bandanna indicated that he was an officer. He duplicated Ole Devil's armament and did not wear his pistol. His black hat lay on the bar, revealing crinkly red hair, and his big, sun-reddened face bore a genially sleepy expression as he raised the schooner to his lips.

"Mr. Blaze!" Ole Devil thundered, striding forward. The sound of his irate voice caused the burly and somnolent-looking young man to give a guilty start and blow out a mouthful of beer. "Just what in hell's name do you think you're doing in here?"

"Why howdy there, Cousin Devil," greeted the recipient of the furious words. He did not attempt to straighten up and he seemed to be on the verge of falling asleep. "Well now, I'm just having me a glass of beer—"

"A *glass of beer!*" Ole Devil spat out, advancing with angry steps that beat time to what he was saying. He came to a halt alongside the bulky object of his wrath. "God damn it, Mr. Blaze, I told you to take the men on mounted drill. So why are you here instead of doing it?"

"Dang it all, Cousin Devil!" Lieutenant Mannen Blaze, second-in-command of Company C, almost wailed as he set down his glass. "You-all made me go along when you took that scout down to Goliad, which's a hell of a distance to ride. So I reckon I'm entitled to take things a mite easy for a spell."

All of the customers and the hotel's three employees who were present had turned their attention to the two young men. While his cousin was speaking, Ole Devil had lifted his hat free. It seemed to the onlookers that he was so disgusted with the feeble excuse he was hard put to control his temper. Letting out an indignant snort, he sent the hat skimming along the top of the bar in the direction of the trio of scouts. Apart from raising his glass so it would not be struck by the head dress, "Deaf" Smith showed an almost complete indifference to what was going on. His companions, who looked like younger versions of himself, duplicated his lack of reaction. Some of the officers from other regiments, remembering what they had heard about the arguing pair, exchanged puzzled glances. When it seemed that one of them was contemplating intervening, the best dressed of the Texians—a tall, slim, impressively handsome man in his middle forties, whose shoulder-long black hair showed not a trace of gray—gave a quick and prohibitive shake of his head, which was obeyed.

Only the dandified group around the table closest to where Ole Devil and Mannen Blaze stood displayed more than a casual interest. As their clothing suggested, the six were well-to-do young Louisianans. They had only recently arrived in San Felipe as members of the one hundred and fifty strong New Orleans' Wildcats, a privately recruited "regiment" of volunteers from the United States. Their families had jointly financed the venture, so each had been given the rank of captain or lieutenant. Newly arrived, none of them had seen action. They were arrogant and self-willed. Filled with a belief in their own importance and abilities, they had already aroused hostility by their condescending attitudes toward the Texians they had come to assist. Watching and listening, they did not trouble to conceal their amused derision over the burly redhead's responses to the questions being fired at him.

"Blast it to hell, *Mister* Blaze!" Ole Devil blared out, looking even more satanic than usual and apparently oblivious to anything other than his errant kinsman. "I've had about enough—"

"Now there's another thing!" Mannen Blaze protested, with something approaching heat, laboriously hoisting his big body erect to confront his cousin. "I'm not so all-fired taken with thishere *"Mister"* talk you're getting real fond of tossing at me. Dadnab it all, Devil, I'm a mite older and a whole heap stronger than you-all so—"

"That doesn't even start to come into it!" Ole Devil roared, still showing no sign of realizing that he and his cousin were arousing speculation by their behavior. Instead, he began to thrust his right forefinger into the broad chest in front of him. "I've been made captain, not you. So you'll do as I damned well tell you. Now get your idle self—"

"Now you-all quit that prodding, damn it!" Mannen bellowed plaintively, before his cousin could conclude the indignant order.

At the table, the six young Creoles threw smirking looks from one to another. To the Jaloux brothers, Captain André and Lieutenant Gérard, Captain Edmond Bardèche, and Lieutenants Jean Mondor, Henri and Marcel Pierre-Quint, the scene they were witnessing only confirmed their suppositions that all Texians were uncouth bores completely bereft of gentlemanly virtues.

Like most of their kind, the six young men had been thoroughly indoctrinated with the *code duello*. To their way of thinking, a gentleman should always be willing to engage an "affair of honor" on the slightest pretext. Each felt that, given similar provocation, family ties would not have prevented him from demanding satisfaction from the satanic-faced newcomer. Not one gave a thought to the fact that Ole Devil and Mannen Blaze had been raised in Louisiana and might have been taught such things. That the burly redhead had not issued a challenge to a duel already filled them with contempt.

"I'll do more than just *prod* you!" Ole Devil threatened, clenching and drawing back the extended hand.

Before Mannen could be struck, acting with a rapidity that formed a vivid contrast to his hitherto lethargic motions, he clamped two enormous hands on the front of his cousin's shirt. Lifting Ole Devil with no more apparent effort than if he had been handling a baby, he gave a surging heave and, swinging around, released his hold. Such was the force he put into his efforts that he propelled his would-be assailant across the room. Although Ole Devil flailed with his arms as an aid to retaining his equilibrium and contrived to hold himself upright, he was unable to halt his progress.

Startled exclamations burst from the Creoles as they realized that the slender Texian was rushing, with little control over his movements, in their direction. Being the nearest of their party to him, the Jaloux brothers tried to stand up and get out of his way. Their attempts were only partially successful. Although they averted an actual collision, neither emerged unscathed.

Half out of his chair, which—like his brother—he had
turned sideways so as to obtain a better view of the quarrel at
the bar, Gérard was caught in the right eye by one of Ole
Devil's wildly waving fists. Nor was the blow gentle, for all that
it had been delivered by accident. Bright lights seemed to erupt
inside his head. Thrown off balance, he measured his length on
the floor. For all that, he fared better than his brother. In his
haste to rise, André tripped and fell. He tried to break his fall,
but landed awkwardly and experienced a searing agony as the
impact sprained his right wrist.

The disruption of the Creoles' group did not end there!

Still unable to restrain his onward momentum, Ole Devil
twisted so that he fell and went rolling across the top of the
table. Hoping to avoid a soaking as their bottle of wine was sent
flying toward him, Bardèche knocked over his chair and fell
backward. Like Gérard Jaloux, Mondor was just commencing
what should have been an evasive action when he, too, received
a punch in the right eye from a hard fist. Instinctively he tried
to jerk away, but felt himself becoming entangled with his
chair. Before he could rectify the situation or regain his balance, he alighted on the unyielding planks with a force that
drove all the breath from his lungs.

Having wreaked havoc upon two more of the party, Ole
Devil continued his passage across the table. Neither Henri nor
Marcel Pierre-Quint were more fortunate than their companions in escaping the disaster. Before they could do more than
start to thrust back and rise from their seats, the Texian
reached them. Rolling over and tumbling into their laps, his
added weight caused the chairs to collapse beneath them. The
brothers let out screeches of Gallic profanity, and they and
their burden went down together. Of the three, Ole Devil came
off best. Impeded by his body, Henri and Marcel were unable to
do much in the way of breaking their falls. So they landed
supine, and the Texian was cushioned from the impact by having them beneath him.

Showing no sign of realizing what he had done, Mannen
came forward to where his cousin and the Pierre-Quint brothers were sprawled. From the way he was behaving, he was so

aroused by the indignities heaped upon him by Ole Devil that
he did not intend to let the matter rest. Apparently he was
more concerned with continuing to vent his injured feelings
than in watching what he was doing. Going past the table, still
moving at speed, he stepped on Henri's right hand as he bent to
hoist Ole Devil erect.

"I warned you-all not to keep a-riling me!" the redhead
yelped, pivoting to swing and push his cousin toward the bar.
In doing so, he ground Henri's fingers between the sole of his
boot and the floor. Ignoring the screech of torment his action
elicited, he went on, "Now I'm going to whomp you good!"

Behind the two Texians, the discomfited Creoles started to
recover from their initial shock. André Jaloux sat nursing his
right wrist and moaning softly. In falling, his brother's head
had hit the floor hard enough to stun him. From the condition
of Gérard's face, he would have difficulty in aiming a pistol for
a few days unless he was able to do so with his left eye.

Hoisting himself painfully into a sitting position, Henri
Pierre-Quint stared at the blood that was running from three
cracked fingernails. He realized that his injuries would prevent
him from holding a pistol or a sword until they healed. Gasping
to replenish his lungs, Mondor levered himself up with the aid
of a chair's seat. Flopping onto it, he gingerly felt his right eye.
It was already discolored and starting to close.

Unharmed, apart from his dignity, Bardèche rose hurriedly.
Without waiting for Marcel Pierre-Quint, who was also standing up and uninjured, he strode to where Ole Devil and Mannen had come to a halt near the bar. Face dark with anger,
Pierre-Quint followed his captain. Each of them had the same
idea in mind. Fistfighting was not their intention. They meant
to issue challenges for formal duels.

Things did not work out the way the Creoles desired.

As Bardèche approached, Ole Devil wrenched himself free
from his cousin's grasp. Having done so, he aimed a blow at the
burly redhead. There was nothing somnolent about the way
Mannen stepped aside, causing Ole Devil to miss him. The
evasion proved to be unfortunate for Bardèche. Although he
saw the Texian's right fist rushing at him, he failed to duplicate

the redhead's avoidance. Struck with considerable violence on
the right cheekbone, he reeled backward. Blood oozed from the
gash opened by the hard knuckles as he tripped and collapsed
onto his rump once more.

Reaching into his jacket for the glove he carried, meaning to
employ it for the traditional challenge, Pierre-Quint was startled by Bardèche's mishap. He came to a halt, but failed to
remove the concealed hand. If he had been longer in Texas, he
would have appreciated that his behavior might be miscon-
strued.

"Don't you-all go pulling no pistol on me!" Mannen bellowed, having seen the Creole's action reflected in the mirror
behind the bar.

Allowing Pierre-Quint no opportunity to correct his erroneous conclusion, the burly redhead swiveled around. Still displaying the kind of alacrity that had characterized all his responses once he was aroused from his state of sloth, he caught
the Creole's right wrist with both his hands. To the recipient of
his attentions, it felt as if the limb was enfolded between the
steel jaws of a bear trap. Although no weapon emerged as Mannen snatched Pierre-Quint's hand into view, he seemed unable
to halt the line of action upon which he had embarked. Instead,
pivoting to his left, he swung his captive in a half circle.

Almost matching Ole Devil in height and build, the young
Creole was no better able than he had been to resist the burly
Texian's enormous strength. So Pierre-Quint found himself being hauled to his right like the weight at the end of a pendulum.
Then, abruptly, his direction was reversed with a wrench that
caused such severe pain that he wondered if his arm had been
torn from its socket. A shrill howl burst from his lips. Instantly
he was released. Twirling away almost gracefully, he struck an
unoccupied table and collapsed, very close to fainting, across
the top of it.

Up to that point none of the room's other occupants had
offered to intervene and help quell the disturbance. Watching
some of the Creoles begin to rise, old "Deaf" Smith made a
gesture to one of the bartenders. Even though no word passed
between them, the man clearly appreciated what was expected

of him. Reaching under the counter, he produced a short blunderbuss, which he passed to the white-haired chief of scouts. As
Smith was taking it, his two companions began to draw the
pistols that were thrust through their waist belts.

"Hold hard there, blast ye!" Smith commanded, swinging the
blunderbuss toward the center of the room and hauling back its
hammer to fully cocked. "This here ain't no seemly bee-hav-ior
for officers 'n' gentlemen."

Strangely, considering the prevailing conditions, Smith and
his men appeared to be aligning their weapons at the Creoles
rather than in the direction of the actual instigators of the disturbance. To André Jaloux, Bardèche, and Mondor and Henri
Pierre-Quint, it seemed that each personally was being men-
aced by the heavy-caliber pistols or the bell-mouthed muzzle of
something far more effective at close quarters.

Equally peculiar was the behavior of the two Texians who
had been responsible for the fracas. Although they were apparently being ignored by the trio of scouts, neither of them appeared to want to continue hostilities against the other.

"My apologies, Colonel Smith," Ole Devil said, striding
smartly across the room to pick up his hat. "With your permission, Mr. Blaze and I will leave."

"It'd likely be's well," the old scout declared.

"Just a moment!" Bardèche put in, taking his hand from the
already badly swollen area where he had been struck and trying
to focus through an eye that resembled a Blue Point oyster
peeping out of its partially open shell. He made as if to advance, but changed his mind as Smith's borrowed blunderbuss
singled him out with disconcerting accuracy. "My friends and I
have been assaulted—"

"It wasn't except by accident," Mannen Blaze protested, re-
lapsing into his earlier attitude of somnolence and ambling over
to retrieve his headgear.

"That doesn't make any difference!" Bardèche spat out indig-
nantly, and his companions muttered their concurrence.
"We've been assaulted and we demand satisfaction."

"Well, now," "Deaf" Smith drawled, looking from one to the other of the offended party, "that's right truthful. 'Cepting, way you've all been hurt, there's none of you'll be able to go fighting no duels for a spell."

3

IT'S YOUR ASSIGNMENT, CAPTAIN HARDIN

"Well, Captain Hardin," greeted Major General Samuel Houston, studying the ramrod-straight young figure standing on the other side of the rickety table that served as a desk in the big wall tent he was using as his quarters and office. Unlike the members of the provisional government, he cared little for his personal comfort. "I don't suppose I need to tell you why I've sent for you, do I?"

"No, sir," Ole Devil Hardin admitted.

Just over an hour had elapsed since the disturbance at the Grand Hotel. Exerting his authority, backed by the solid argument of his borrowed blunderbuss, "Deaf" Smith had insisted that the two parties concerned should not remain in each other's presence. So Ole Devil and Lieutenant Mannen Blaze had taken their departure while the injuries of the six Creoles were receiving treatment.

Once outside the building, instead of continuing their quarrel, the two cousins appeared to have forgotten their differences. They were on the best of terms by the time they had reached the Texas Light Cavalry's tent lines, and the subject of the mounted drill was not mentioned. Nor, when the captain had given instructions that would involve his lethargic-looking lieutenant in some strenuous activity, did Mannen repeat his earlier complaints or show any sign of shirking the duty. Rather he had set about it with a lively cheerfulness that seemed at odds with his general behavior. It was noticeable that the men to whom he began to issue orders showed no surprise over the way he was acting.

Neither Ole Devil nor his cousin had been particularly surprised when the former had received a summons to report immediately to the general's headquarters. Leaving Mannen to carry out the preparations he had ordered, the captain made his way to Houston. Having anticipated the summons, he had tidied up his appearance, and the Manton pistol now rode in its loop on his belt.

If the young Texian had any doubts over why he had been summoned, they ended upon his arrival. As he had expected, on entering the big wall tent he found that General Houston was not alone. "Deaf" Smith was standing alongside Ole Devil's uncle, Colonel Edward Fog. Although they had not met, the Texian had no need to exercise his mental powers greatly to deduce the identity of the fourth man at the general's table-desk.

Something above medium height, stoutish, in his early fifties, with the blue-jowled features of a Provençal Frenchman, there was little of the Creoles' dandified elegance about him, although he was dressed in the same Creole fashion. For all that, he was the commanding officer of the New Orleans Wildcats— Colonel Jules Dumoulin. He had a hard-bitten, disciplined appearance that told of military experience and suggested he had been a professional soldier for a number of years. There was nothing in his expression or attitude to suggest what he might be thinking about the injuries suffered by his subordinates.

However, Ole Devil's main attention was reserved for the person to whom he had come to report.

Big, powerfully built, with longish and almost white hair, the commanding general of the Republic of Texas's army made an imposing figure even when seated in such simple and primitive surroundings. He was the kind of man who had no need of pomp and splendor to enhance his authority; his personality did all that was necessary in that respect. Although his seamed, lined, and Indian-dark face rarely showed emotion, his surprisingly young-looking blue eyes suggested a deep inner strength. There was something about him, the undefinable—yet instantly recognizable—aura of one who was born with the gift of leadership.

Since the withdrawal to the east had commenced, Houston had packed away his uniform's formal dress tunic and black bicorn chapeau. They had been replaced by a waist-long, fringed buckskin jacket, a tightly rolled scarlet silk bandanna, an open-necked dark-blue worsted shirt, and a broad-brimmed white "planter's" hat, which were better suited to his needs. Since his tan-colored riding breeches and shining black Wellington boots[1] were purely functional, he still retained them.

One point had struck Ole Devil as soon as he had entered the tent. Although he was aware of why he had been summoned, the general was bareheaded. The hat lay with a brace of pistols and a saber on the bed in the rear portion of the structure.

"Is that *all* you have to say?" demanded the smallish yet excellently developed blond-haired Colonel Fog when his nephew relapsed into silence after the brief answer.

"No excuse, sir," Ole Devil replied, staring straight ahead.

"Blast it!" Colonel Fog exclaimed. "I'll expect some better reason than that."

"No excuse, sir!" Ole Devil repeated, conscious that Dumoulin was watching him.

"Aw shucks, now, Ed," Smith protested placatingly. "Like I told the colonel here, all of those boys of his'n got hurt accidental like. Mind you, I can't say's how I blames young Mannen for getting riled, way Devil here was a-riding him. Trouble being, he's so all-fired big, he just don't know his own strength."

"And, as I stated, I am willing to accept that explanation,"

---

1. Wellington boots: In this context, not the modern, waterproof variety. Instead they are the style, with high legs covering the leg as far as the knee in front and cut away behind, made popular during the Napoleonic wars by the Duke of Wellington.—J.T.E.

the Frenchman went on, his tones harsh without being in any way hostile. "The whole affair was lamentable and should never have happened. However, as it did, we can do nothing except try to ensure it goes no farther."

"I'm in complete agreement with *that,* Colonel," Ole Devil's uncle stated grimly. "And I can assure you it will not, as far as the Texas Light Cavalry is concerned." His gaze turned to his nephew, and he continued, "Company C is to be detached on special duty, Captain Hardin. They will leave tomorrow at dawn."

"Yes, sir," Ole Devil responded, still conscious of Dumoulin's scrutiny. "They'll be ready."

"May I have your permission to depart, sir?" the Frenchman requested, after giving what might have been a nod of approval for the young Texian's unhesitating acceptance of his superior's orders. "As my regiment will also be leaving in the morning, I have many things demanding my attention."

"You may go, Colonel," Houston authorized.

"My thanks for being so understanding—Jules," Colonel Fog said, stepping around the table and behind the general.

"It is regrettable that the need should have arisen—Edward," Dumoulin answered, accepting and shaking the small Texian's hand. *"Au revoir,* gentlemen." His gaze once again swung in Ole Devil's direction, and he went on, "May our next meeting be in more pleasant circumstances, Captain Hardin."

"Thank you, sir," the young Texian replied, still unable to detect any trace of the other's sentiments, but believing they were favorable to him. "I'll do my best to make sure that it is."

Throwing a smart salute to Houston, the Frenchman turned and strode from the Texian's presence without a backward glance.

"He ain't such a bad hombre, considering he's a Frog," Smith commented after Dumoulin had gone beyond earshot. "I'd've thought he'd start to screech like a knife-struck hawg when you told him's he'd got to take his soldier-boys down to Harrisburg and guard good old Davey Burnet's bunch."

"Well, he didn't," Houston answered, eyeing his lanky chief of scouts sardonically. "And now, *if* it's all right with *you,* I'd like to hear from Captain Hardin not *how* but *why* all those remarkable *accidental* injuries happened."

"With all respect, sir," Ole Devil said, showing no more emotion than was being expressed by the three older men. "No excuse."

"It wouldn't have had any connection with the way in which those six young foo—*gentlemen* from New Orleans have been casting doubts on the courage of an officer under your command," the general suggested, "would it?"

"Again, with respect, sir," Ole Devil began, his voice unemotionally polite. "I can't add anything to—"

"Very well, captain," Houston interrupted, drumming his fingers on the top of the table for a moment. There was a frosty glint in his eyes as he started to speak again. "I'm not an overinquisitive man, nor do I have a suspicious nature." He darted a glare at Smith, who gave a muted snort of disbelief. "However, I do try to keep in touch with *everything* that goes on in my command—"

"That's another way of saying he's nosy," the old chief of scouts explained sotto voce.

"For instance," the general continued, as if he had not heard Smith. "I've been told that, because Lieutenant Paul Dimmock was fortunate enough to have escaped from the massacre at Goliad, certain of our esteemed supporters from New Orleans have raised what might be considered doubts regarding his personal courage and integrity. Not unnaturally he is said to be taking very grave exception to such imputations."

"That's a real fancy way of putting it," Smith drawled. "But he sure's hell can't be blamed happen he's getting riled over what they're saying."

"Where is Mr. Dimmock now, by the way?" Houston inquired, taking no more notice than he had of the scout's previous comment.

"I sent him out in command of a foraging detail, sir," Ole Devil explained. "He won't be back before nightfall, if then."

"And while he's away," Houston said drily, "you have a quarrel with the second-in-command of your company that has resulted in every one of the men Mr. Dimmock might have wished to challenge to a duel being, at least temporarily, rendered incapable of fighting one."

"There's some's might say, knowing how touchy these here young hotheads both Texian 'n' Louisianan can get where their honor's concerned, that it's right lucky they can't," Smith declared, with deceptive mildness and oozing innocence. "Anyways, those fancy-Dans was tolerable unlucky getting in the way like they did."

"So *you* told Colonel Dumoulin," Houston growled.

"Way he talked," Smith pointed out, "he knowed I was telling the truth."

"That's because he's new here from New Orleans," the general answered, but his tone robbed the words of any sting. "Anybody who's been around Texas for a spell would look to see if the calendar had been changed if you told them Monday came a day before Tuesday. However, whether he believed you or not, he's content to have the whole affair forgotten, and that's what I'd like to have happen too."

"Let's hope them hotheads of his'n see it that way," Smith drawled.

"I'm relying on him to see that they do," Houston replied. "Anyway, we're lucky that Governor Burnet's asked for extra troops to guard the 'temporary capital' and that Urrea is down in the southeast. It gives me an excuse to send the New Orleans Wildcats there without making it look as if I'm trying to get rid of them."

"It helps with what you've got in mind for young Devil here, comes to that," Smith remarked, looking pointedly at the rigid young Texian. "Does he *have* to stand like that, Sam?"

"At ease, Captain Hardin," Houston ordered. "As Colonel Fog told you, your company is to leave in the morning. They'll go to Washington-on-the-Brazos and, with my written authority, once again assume responsibility for the safekeeping of the consignment of caplocks. Your men will bring them to Groce's and, having done so, stay there and await the arrival of the rest of the army."

Up to that point Ole Devil had been listening to the general with a sense of relief. It had been apparent that Houston, his uncle, and Colonel Dumoulin had not only understood but approved of the motives behind the "quarrel" that he had had with Mannen Blaze at the Grand Hotel. Aware that Lieutenant Dimmock was being provoked by the Creoles' unjustified insinuations, he had taken steps to avert a confrontation. On learning from "Deaf" Smith and another of the general's stoutest supporters—who had shared his apprehensions over the consequences of trouble between Dimmock and the young Louisianans—where they were to be found, he had formulated a scheme. By good luck it had succeeded with far less difficulty than he had anticipated.

Furthermore Ole Devil's assumption of how Houston would react had been correct. He had expected that steps would be taken to separate the two parties before the Creoles were able to participate in "affairs of honor." This had happened, but he had noticed that the general had said *they* rather than *you* when speaking of the duty to which his company had been assigned. He also realized that although the matter of the trouble with the New Orleans Wildcats had been resolved, his uncle was still looking perturbed. The emotion, he felt sure, did not stem from concern or disapproval over the trouble with the Creoles.

"Groce's, sir," Ole Devil repeated. "But that's north of here, and Harrisburg's thirty miles or so to the southeast."

"I *have* been known to look at a map of Texas on occasion, Captain," Houston answered, understanding what had provoked the comment. As far as the majority of his army and the members of the provisional government were aware, the route of the withdrawal was directed toward the temporary capital. "Nevertheless those are the orders your company will carry out."

"But I won't be with them, sir?" Ole Devil guessed.

"That depends upon whether you are willing to volunteer for a very special duty," the general said quietly, and the faces of the two older men behind him grew even more grave. He raised his right hand as the young Texian was about to speak. "However, as it is an exceptionally hazardous mission and as there is every possibility that whoever attempts it will be killed, or captured—which amounts to the same, except it would be a slower death—I want to tell you what it is before you give me your answer."

Long before Houston's explanation of what would be expected of him was concluded, Ole Devil realized that the danger involved in carrying out the mission had not been overexaggerated. What was more, he knew that he had not merely been sent for to explain his behavior at the hotel. That aspect had been settled satisfactorily before his arrival. The assignment that he was being offered, fantastic as it might appear on the surface, was one of the greatest importance. If it was successful, the effects could be as far-reaching as the general hoped.

"It's a big gamble, Devil," Colonel Fog commented after Houston had stopped speaking. "I'll not deny that the odds are greatly against it succeeding. But, if it does, at the very least we'll gain a badly needed respite."

"We'll gain far more than that," Ole Devil replied, at last understanding his uncle's concern for his welfare. "And it will work, if all I've heard about Santa Anna's character is true."

"He's one mean, ornery, vengeful son of a bitch, for sure," Smith declared. "Happen that be what you've heard."

"Something along those lines," Ole Devil conceded, without taking his gaze from Houston. "What has the government said about your idea, sir?"

"It hasn't been mentioned to them, and by the time they find out, they'll have other things to occupy them," Houston replied, and Smith, no lover of politicians, gave an appreciative chuckle. Opening the drawer of his table, the general took out an impressive-looking document. It had a printed heading, a written message, and a large red seal. "This is the Republic of Texas's stationery and seal, which were sent to me just before the 'Runaway Scrape.' I was instructed to use them in future for all official communications. So that's what I'm doing."

"Only not the way they was counting on," Smith cackled delightedly as the young Texian accepted and started to read the document. "But it's being put to a good use."

"I shouldn't think that Santa Anna is familiar with President Burnet's signature," Houston remarked, after Ole Devil had completed his examination and handed back the sheet of paper.

"And, provided it is delivered in an appropriate manner, it's unlikely that he will bother taking the time to find out whether it's a forgery."

"That's for sure," Smith seconded. "Happen it's got to him the right way, Devil-boy, he's going to be so pot-boiling mad that he won't care about nothing 'cept getting evens with the feller's he thinks's sent it."

"Well," said Houston, "will you accept the assignment, Captain Hardin?"

"Yes, sir," Ole Devil replied, holding his voice just as even. "And I'll do my best to see it through."

"We know you will," Houston declared, and Smith nodded in agreement.

"It's not a one-man assignment, Devil," Colonel Fog pointed out, studying his nephew and thinking of the terrible risks that would be necessary if the scheme was to be brought to a successful conclusion.

"I'd go along with you, boy," Smith continued, "but it can't be done. You can have your pick of my fellers, though."

"*Gracias,* sir, but that won't be necessary," Ole Devil answered. He glanced at his uncle, "With your permission, sir, I'll take Tommy Okasi—"

"I thought you would," Colonel Fog admitted before the captain could finish. "You couldn't have chosen a better man. Who else?"

"Just one more," Ole Devil drawled. "Paul Dimmock."

"Dimmock?" Colonel Fog repeated.

"Yes, sir," Ole Devil confirmed. "We all know that he's no coward, and the fact that he's been on an assignment like this ought to settle any doubts other people might have about him."

"You'll not be able to tell them what's happened when you come back," Houston warned. "At least not until we're able to show proof that it's been successful."

"I appreciate *that,* sir," Ole Devil stated. "But by taking Paul I'll show him that I and, more important, *you* have no doubts about his courage."

"That's all very well, Devil," Colonel Fog remarked. "But he might do something reckless to try to prove how brave he is."

"Not while he's with me, sir," Ole Devil contradicted. "He knows I don't doubt him. And I'd rather have him where I can keep an eye on him than leave him with the company. He's growing increasingly touchy, and in my opinion it'll be better for all concerned if he's kept occupied. On top of that he knows the country between here and Santa Anna's column better than I do."

"It's your assignment, Captain Hardin," Houston declared, nodding in grim approval. The young Texian's summation strengthened his belief that he had selected the best man for the task. "So I'm not going to try to tell you who to take, or how it should be done. All I can say is go and do it any way you see fit."

"Thank you, sir," Ole Devil responded, hoping that he was not showing the pride and satisfaction he was feeling. "When shall we leave?"

"Can you be on your way before noon tomorrow?" Houston wanted to know.

"Easily, sir," Ole Devil promised. "Something told me that we'd be sent out on a patrol after that trouble at the hotel—"

"Something, or *somebody?*" the general growled, glancing at his chief of scouts, who assumed a far from convincing air of injured innocence.

"It seemed likely that you'd want to separate us from the Wildcats until tempers cooled down a mite, sir," Ole Devil countered. He and Smith had envisaged this possibility during their discussion on how to deal with the situation that had arisen between the Creoles and Dimmock. "So I told Mr. Blaze to start making ready to leave, and I sent Sergeant Smith to fetch back the foraging detail."

"Smart thinking," the general said in praise. "Now, Captain, only we four here know what I'm sending you to do. You'll have to tell Mr. Dimmock and that man of yours—"

"May I tell Mangrove Hallistead, sir?" Ole Devil put in. "There are a couple of things he might be able to help me with."

"I trust him, but don't tell him any more than is absolutely necessary," Houston replied. "It's imperative that no mention of this gets out, and I don't mean just so Santa Anna doesn't hear about it. None of our people must know. I don't need to explain why, do I?"

"No, sir!" Ole Devil stated, and the grin that came to his face made it seem even more satanic. "The government aren't going to be any too pleased if they learn what you could be letting them in for. Of course by the time they find out, it would be too late for them to try to stop it. But it's still better that they don't hear until it's over."

"You're not wrong about *that,* boy," Smith chuckled, savoring the thought of how the politicians at Harrisburg would react if they were aware of Houston's scheme. "What they don't know won't cause 'em to lose sleep at nights, nor make fuss for us fellers who're doing the fighting."

"Is there anything else you need me for, sir?" Ole Devil asked, deciding that his uncle and the general shared, even if they did not express, similar sentiments to those of the old scout. "I've some extra preparations to make now I've been given this assignment."

"Go and do what needs doing, boy. And if you need anything, don't hesitate to ask for it," Houston authorized. "You can collect your company's orders and this document in the morning."

"Yo!" Ole Devil said, saluting as he gave what had already come to be accepted as the cavalryman's response to a command.

"Good luck, boy," Smith drawled and, after the young captain had left, he continued grimly, "That's one hell of a wild notion you've come up with, Sam. But, like I said when you told me about it, if anybody can pull it off, he can."

"I'll have sent him to his death if he can't," Houston answered quietly. "And the damnable thing about it is that he might still pull it off by getting killed."

4

YOU'LL GET YOUR SATISFACTION

"M'sieur Hardin!" called a young voice that carried what seemed to be a quiver of nervous tension. "I wish to have a word with you!"

Noticing the way in which his name had been spoken, Ole Devil Hardin had a premonition of what was coming. Turning his attention away from the man to whom he had been talking, he looked to see where the words had originated. Even before his gaze reached the three figures who were emerging from the front entrance of the Grand Hotel, his ears identified the speaker's accent.

It was that of a well-educated Creole!

Although the Texian recognized lieutenants Gérard Jaloux and Marcel Pierre-Quint, members of the party with whom he had earlier been in conflict, the way they were behaving informed him that they had not spoken. They were walking slowly, allowing their companion to draw ahead of them.

Somewhat shorter and more stockily built than either Jaloux or Pierre-Quint, the third member of the group had not been with them in the hotel's barroom. However, his attire suggested that he was another member of the New Orleans Wildcats. In his late teens, he was younger than his companions and had grown a mustache in the hope of creating the impression that he was older. Possibly for the same reason, he had conformed to the Texians' habit of going armed. There was a fine-looking caplock pistol tucked into his trousers' waistband. While he moved with a stiff and purposeful erectness, to Ole Devil's experienced gaze his posture suggested a tension similar to that which had tinged his voice.

An annoyed hiss burst from the Texian as, coming to a halt, he took in the sight. The last thing he wanted, with matters of importance demanding his full attention, was a further altercation with the Creoles.

After being dismissed from Major General Samuel Houston's office, Ole Devil had returned to his own quarters in a pensive frame of mind. On his arrival he had relieved Lieutenant Mannen Blaze's anxiety over the result of the interview. Then he had told his cousin of the task to which Company C had been assigned and also that he would not be accompanying them to carry it out. That he refrained from mentioning the nature of his own mission did not imply a lack of faith in the burly redhead's discretion. He knew that Mannen was completely reliable and would not speak of it. However, he had been ordered to limit the number of people to whom he divulged the details, and that was sufficient to ensure his reticence.

Nor, in spite of being curious, had the redhead attempted to elicit the information. No matter how he generally looked and behaved in public, he was anything but the somnolent dullard he frequently pretended to be. His long association with Ole Devil suggested that there was something of greater importance than a routine scouting mission that was going to separate him from the company. Appreciating also that his cousin would have told him if it was permissible, he was content to carry out his own orders and have his superior officer—for whom, his comments at the hotel notwithstanding, he had the greatest respect, admiration, and affection—to do whatever was required elsewhere.

Although Ole Devil had not been able to take Mannen into his confidence, he had realized it was advisable, in fact necessary, to tell Tommy Okasi what they were being sent to do.

On the surface the Texian's first choice of a companion for such an important and perilous venture seemed to have no justification.

Under five feet six inches in height, although possessing a sturdy physical development, Tommy Okasi did not look impressive. In his early twenties, with a sallow complexion and almond eyes, his features betrayed Oriental blood. He rarely wore a hat, and his black hair was kept closely cropped. His garments consisted of a loose-fitting black shirt hanging outside baggy trousers of the same material, which were tucked into matching Hessian boots. Even the pair of long-hilted, slightly curved swords with small circular guards that were dangling— the shorter one at the right—by slings attached to his broad leather waist belt did little to explain the reason for his selection.

As there was only limited contact between his homeland, Japan, and the Western Hemisphere at that period, Tommy was generally assumed to be Chinese. Many people expected him to display a meekness similar to that of members of the latter race. Nor, unless he was provoked or some other need arose, did he do anything to disillusion them.

However, although for personal reasons Tommy no longer retained the traditional costume and hairstyle, he was a fully trained samurai[1] warrior. In spite of his willingness to be regarded as no more than Ole Devil's valet, his martial education made him a very effective fighting man who was able to offer useful suggestions on how to succeed in their various missions.

Knowing that the Mexicans employed spies and wanting to avoid any chance of being overheard while they were talking, Ole Devil had left the organization and preparations for their departure in his cousin's capable hands. As he and Tommy strolled together in search of the man he wished to consult, he passed on the details of their unusual and dangerous assignment. They had been told that Mangrove Hallistead was staying at the Grand Hotel and they were making their way there.

1. Details of Tommy Okasi's background and weapons are given in Appendix A.—J.T.E.

Remembering Colonel Dumoulin's assurances and knowing that the New Orleans Wildcats were camped on the other side of the town, the Texian did not consider the possibility of meeting any of them. The interruption came while Tommy was suggesting that they might achieve their purpose by utilizing his skill as an archer and employing some of the specialized arrows peculiar to his nation.

"Well?" Ole Devil asked, employing a coldly forbidding tone that would have served as a warning to anybody who had been acquainted with him for even a short time. Tommy, who knew him very well, glanced at him and drew back a couple of steps. "What can I do for you?"

While speaking, the Texian devoted some of his attention to the two older Creoles. He noticed that although neither had been armed at the earlier meeting, they had now remedied the situation. Each had the épée type of sword hanging from the military-style belt he was wearing and had a pistol tucked through it. Most significantly the firearms were obviously a matched pair. Like the swords, they had been designed for a more specific purpose than mere defense.

"My name is Alphonse Jules Dumoulin, m'sieur," the youngster answered, advancing another four paces after his companions had stopped. "I am a lieutenant in the New Orleans Wildcats." His words were coming out in a jerky fashion, almost as if he was repeating something that he had been instructed to say. "It has been brought to my notice that you assaulted several of my brother officers and comrades-in-arms—"

"'As it also been brought to your notice, *lieutenant*, that your colonel has received an explanation? He accepts that the incident was a regrettable accident and, as such, in the interests of the cause for which we are fighting, should be forgotten by all concerned." Ole Devil could see that his words were having a disturbing effect upon the youngster, who, he guessed, was closely related to the commanding officer of the New Orleans Wildcats. "Furthermore, if your brother officers and comrades-in-arms desire to continue the issue contrary to your superior's *instructions,* don't you consider that it should be for them to do so personally?"

"As you can see, sir," Dumoulin answered, turning slightly to indicate Jaloux's completely closed right eye and the sling supporting Pierre-Quint's right arm, "they are temporarily unable to demand satisfaction and know you would not wish to take advantage of their incapacitation. So, as we have heard that, like ourselves, you are leaving for an indefinite period, we feel that you should grant them satisfaction. As the honor of our regiment is involved, I have been selected to represent them."

"Have you?" Ole Devil said, after what seemed to Dumoulin a *very* extended period of silence. His voice was as chilling as the inside of an icehouse.

For all his desire to display the composure that he believed was expected of a grown man in such conditions, the Creole youngster was feeling increasingly perturbed. Somehow the confrontation was not progressing as his companions had told him it would. To hear them talk, delivering a challenge was an exhilarating and noble experience, the ultimate test of manhood.

Dumoulin discovered that he felt neither exhilarated nor noble. Instead there was something distinctly unnerving about the grim-looking Texian who stood before him. He found that it was almost impossible to meet the steely scrutiny of those hard, dark eyes, and he wished that he could turn to Jaloux or Pierre-Quint for guidance. Wondering if the sensation was the result of cowardice on his part, he felt a growing anger with himself. He became filled with a determination to carry the affair through to the bitter end.

"I have, m'sieur!" the youngster confirmed, hoping that he was sounding more resolute than he was feeling. He tensed, right hand clenching and opening spasmodically, conscious of his companions watching his every move. In spite of his inclination, pride forced him to continue. "I trust that as a gentleman you will not need me to make my point more forcibly?"

For his part, although nothing showed externally, Ole Devil was fuming with rage. Faced as he was with the need to make ready for the dangerous and potentially important assignment he had been given, the last thing he wanted was to have such a distraction thrust upon him. Yet he realized that, having allowed it to develop so far, it would be practically impossible to avoid the issue.

Born and raised in Louisiana, Ole Devil had had considerable experience with the arrogant and race-proud French-Creoles' creed of *code duello,* although so far he had not become involved in it. To use his military rank as a means of refusing the challenge, particularly as Dumoulin had said *m'sieur* instead of *Captain* would avail him nothing. Clearly the youngster had been persuaded by his older companions to represent them, and he felt he had to do so. While his heart might not be in it, he would be unwilling to let it appear he was afraid to fight. In such a frame of mind, he might make matters worse by striking Ole Devil as a means of ensuring the duel took place.

"Very well, m'sieur," the Texian barked, accepting the inevitable and cracking out each word with savage finality. "You'll have your satisfaction!"

Having attained the result he wanted, Dumoulin discovered that his success was more disconcerting than satisfying. Nor was his condition improved by an uneasy suspicion that he was behaving in a foolish and irresponsible manner.

Although the youngster came from a similar social background, his upbringing had differed in one important respect from that of his companions; his father, one of the leading members of the medical profession in Louisiana, had never encouraged him to adopt the generally accepted sentiments regarding the worthiness of the *code duello.* In fact, both publicly as well as in private, Dr. Charles Alphonse Dumoulin had never referred to the participants in trivial so-called affairs of honor with anything but disparaging terms.

Bored with waiting to commence his medical education, Dumoulin had persuaded his parents to let him accompany his Uncle Jules and friends to Texas. Wondering if his father's views on dueling had affected his courage, he waited for an opportunity to prove himself. Like the rest of the New Orleans

Wildcats' younger officers, he found the situation vastly different from what he had expected. Instead of being dispatched immediately to engage the enemy, the Wildcats were informed that they would accompany the Republic of Texas's Army in its withdrawal. Disappointment and boredom had had an adverse effect upon the hotheaded young bloods who had come in search of adventure. Now they were beginning to wax critical of the Texians. Nor had their mood been improved by learning that Colonel James Walker Fannin's command had been massacred at Goliad and that, in spite of their offers of action, General Houston had refused to permit any punitive expeditions.

To do Dumoulin justice, he had never subscribed to some of his companions' suggestions that Lieutenant Paul Dimmock's survival indicated a lack of courage. However, without realizing what was happening, he found himself becoming involved in the issue.

Shortly after Colonel Dumoulin had spoken to his officers about the incident at the Grand Hotel, declaring his disapproval and warning that the matter must not be taken any further, the youngster had been invited by Jaloux and Pierre-Quint to accompany them for a drink. As there had been nothing else for him to do, the preparations for moving out being left in the hands of the regiment's servants, he had accepted.

On arriving at the hotel, it had soon become apparent to the youngster that his companions did not intend to respect their commanding officer's wishes. What was more, as their injuries prevented them from competing with a man who had such a high reputation as a handler of weapons, Dumoulin found that they expected him to avenge what they had described as an affront to the honor of their regiment. Although he had hoped to avoid the issue, without making it appear that he was afraid —some of their comments had implied that his own courage was in question—they had seen the cause of their hostility approaching. Faced with his companions' obvious expectations, his pride would not allow him to refuse when they had stated that he should go outside and demand satisfaction.

"Thank you, sir," Dumoulin responded after a moment's pause, feeling as if his throat was becoming blocked up. Struggling to control the growing alarm and consternation that were assailing him, he saw what might be a way out. "My seconds will await your convenience in the morning."

And that, the youngster told himself with something close to relief, was that. It was over, for the time being at least. Perhaps, on learning what had happened, his uncle would make an official intervention and prevent the duel from taking place.

There was an unpleasant surprise to come!

"No, m'sieur," Ole Devil contradicted, still watching Dumoulin with the same disconcertingly steady gaze. "We'll settle it right now!"

"N—*Now?*" the youngster almost yelped, and he heard his companions let out soft-spoken exclamations of satisfaction.

"Now!" Ole Devil confirmed, apparently devoting his entire attention to his challenger, but also keeping the other two Creoles under observation and drawing conclusions from their reactions. "As you said, m'sieur, I'm taking my company out on patrol in the morning and won't have time to spare for meeting you before I leave. So, unless *you* have any objections, now is satisfactory for me."

"B—But—!" Dumoulin spluttered.

"Being the challenged party, I believe the choice of weapons is mine," Ole Devil continued remorselessly, showing no sign of having heard the interruption or noticing the youngster's growing perturbation. "I choose pistols—"

"Excuse me, Cap—M'sieur Hardin," Dumoulin interrupted, seeing hope of gaining a respite. "Under the circumstances, our affair must proceed according to the accepted conventions. Your choice must be communicated by your seconds."

"That is correct, m'sieur," Ole Devil admitted. He saw Jaloux and Pierre-Quint look annoyed. He looked past them and went on, "Will you oblige by acting for me, Captain Hallistead?"

"Certainly, Captain Hardin," replied a well-modulated and cultured voice with the carrying resonance of one who was used to speaking in public and making himself heard.

Looking over their shoulders, the Creoles studied the speaker as he strolled from the front door of the hotel. There was something flamboyant, almost theatrical, about his tall beaver hat and well-cut riding clothes. If Jaloux and Pierre-Quint had been more observant, they would have remembered that he was present during the earlier contretemps. He had in fact prevented another of the onlookers from making a comment that could have ruined Ole Devil's plan. The trio regarded him with different feelings. To the injured young men, he offered a means of obtaining revenge. Dumoulin saw him as an interfering busybody.

"Gentlemen," Ole Devil said. "May I present Captain Mangrove Hallistead of General Houston's staff."

"Who else is acting for you?" Dumoulin inquired before the introduction could be acknowledged.

"My companion," the Texian replied, indicating Tommy Okasi.

"Your *companion!*" the youngster repeated, darting a look at the Oriental and, in spite of their eagerness to bring about the duel, the other two Creoles showed a similar surprise. "But he's only a *Chinaman—!*"

"Japanese," Hallistead corrected before Ole Devil could do so, "An Oriental race, true, but in no way contiguous with the Celestial Empire of Ancient Cathay. Furthermore, in his native land Mr. Okasi is what is termed a samurai. They are an elite warrior class and of the lower nobility. By our standards his rank would be that of baronet. In fact, gentlemen, as this is the case, he will have to waive the question of his birthright if he is willing to act for Captain Hardin."

Such was the magnificent authority with which the pronouncement was made that the Creoles were visibly impressed. All of them had heard of Mangrove Hallistead. Prior to his departure for Texas, he had appeared with resounding success at the best theaters in every major city of the United States. Such was the fame he had achieved that, notwithstanding the general reluctance shown by many wealthy families to accept members of the theatrical profession as social equals, he had

had entry to the majority of influential households on both sides of the Mason-Dixon line.[2]

One of the conventions for the conducting of a duel required that the seconds be of equal status in society with the principals they were to attend. However, provided a man was willing to waive the question of his rank, he could act for a friend of lower social standing.

Bearing in mind who they were dealing with, the Creoles—particularly Jaloux and Pierre-Quint—were willing to concede Hallistead's point regarding the eligibility of Tommy Okasi acting as the Texian's second. While Dumoulin wanted to protest, he believed such an act would make the men around him think he was afraid. So he kept silent and allowed his companions to continue with the arrangements.

"Very well, sir," Pierre-Quint said, glancing at and receiving a confirmatory nod from Jaloux, but not bothering to consult with his principal. "If this—gentleman—is in agreement—"

"I am," confirmed Tommy, who spoke English well enough to have followed the conversation and knew what was expected of him.

"Then, gentlemen," Pierre-Quint went on, making no attempt to conceal his satisfaction, "if you will accompany us a short way along the street, we can make the necessary arrangements."

Watching the four men walk past him, Ole Devil looked at Dumoulin and almost felt sorry for him. His face had lost most of its color, and he seemed to be on the point of calling to his seconds. Then, noticing that he was being observed by the Texian, he stiffened and set his teeth. Swinging on his heel, he began to stare with great intensity at the window of the general store—from which all the merchandise had been removed—across the street.

2. Mason-Dixon line: Sometimes erroneously called the Mason-Dixie line. The boundary between Maryland and Pennsylvania, as surveyed in 1763–67 by the Englishmen Charles Mason and Jeremiah Dixon, which had already come to be regarded as the line dividing Southern slave and Northern free states.—J.T.E.

Deciding that there was nothing to be gained by speaking to Dumoulin, Ole Devil did not offer to do so. Instead, he listened to the seconds. They had not bothered to move away and, particularly as Hallistead—whose voice had been trained to be audible at long distance—was doing most of the talking, he could hear what was being said.

By the time the arrangements were concluded, the Texian realized there were a number of irregularities being permitted in the conducting of the duel. If it should end in a fatality, these would cause serious repercussions for all concerned and especially for the surviving principal.

5

THERE MUST BE ANOTHER SHOT

"In addition to being gentlemen of honor, we are also holding commissions as officers and we are on active service in time of war," announced Mangrove Hallistead, acting as spokesman for Ole Devil Hardin's faction, as he looked from Tommy Okasi to lieutenants Marcel Pierre-Quint and Gérard Jaloux. "So I assume we are *all* in agreement that our military duties must take precedence over our private affairs?"

"Well—yes—that is correct," Pierre-Quint conceded somewhat dubiously, after having traded looks with Jaloux and noticing that the Oriental had nodded concurrence. In his capacity as Alphonse Jules Dumoulin's senior second he continued, "But an affair of honor is an obligation that cannot be overlooked."

"Naturally. And nobody wishes it to be," the entertainer admitted majestically. "However while circumstances, the nature of which we are all cognizant of, do not permit us to adhere rigidly to the Clonmel Code,[1] it is imperative that we employ its twentieth commandment, to wit, 'Seconds are bound

1. Clonmel Code: Twenty-six "commandments" laying down the rules and procedures to be followed when fighting a duel, primarily with pistols,

to attempt a reconciliation before any meeting takes place.' "
For all his insistence, he refrained from completing the ruling
with the words "or after a sufficient firing or hits as specified,"
but concluded, "Don't you agree, gentlemen?"

"We agree," Pierre-Quint said reluctantly, once again glancing at his companion. They were both so impressed by Hallistead's assured demeanor and knowledge that neither wished to
admit that he was not equally conversant with the various
"commandments" of the Clonmel Code. "However, in our case
this would be a waste of time. We know our principal is adamant and will refuse any offer of a reconciliation until his
honor has been satisfied."

"Very well," the entertainer acceded, although a strict adherence to the Clonmel Code would have required that an attempt
be at least made. "Our principal has stated that his choice of
weapons is pistols. Is this satisfactory?"

"It is," Pierre-Quint affirmed, laying his hand on the butt of
the firearm in his belt. "We anticipated the need and have
brought a pair with us. They can be used, unless your principal
has any objections."

"He has none," Hallistead declared, duplicating Ole Devil's
summation that the weapons in question were a matched brace
of dueling pistols. "And now to the venue. There is an area a
short distance beyond the livery barn that will offer us the
necessary seclusion and privacy. I would suggest that we wend
our way thence and let the affair be settled without delay."

"We're agreeable," Pierre-Quint declared, ignoring the fact
that by convention an independent director of the duel and a
surgeon should be present. Instead he threw a look of triumph
at Jaloux and, glancing around him at the street, went on, "The
sooner it's settled, the less chance of intervention."

Although there were a number of people in the vicinity, some
of whom glanced at the group in passing, nobody offered to
stop and address them. The majority of the men guessed what
was taking place, but accepted that it was none of their con-

---

adopted by the Summer Assizes at Clonmel, County Tipperary, Ireland, in
1770.—J.T.E.

cern. Duels were sufficiently common in the United States and
Texas for them to appreciate the danger of displaying too much
interest, much less actually trying to interfere in the proceedings.

Separating without further conversation, the seconds joined
their principals. Once again the two older Creoles' eagerness to
commence was noticeable. Instead of telling Dumoulin what
had been arranged, in order to ascertain his feelings they took
him by the arms and set off toward the alley at the end of the
Grand Hotel. Following them, Hallistead explained the arrangements to Ole Devil and gave further information that
added to the suppositions he had already formulated.

On arriving, the party found that the spot selected by the
entertainer was perfect for their purpose. While less than a
quarter of a mile from the livery barn, the hollow into which
they descended was sufficiently large and deep for the duel to
take place without it being observed by anybody beyond the
rim. Considering the various irregularities they were permitting
in the affair, they all felt this to be of some importance.

As it was desirable to avoid proceedings taking place while in
the heat of temper, one rule that all of the various conventions
laid down was that there should, if possible, be a period of
waiting between the challenge and the event. However, they
also took into account that circumstances might render this
impractical. So the duel following shortly after the challenge
was permissible under the prevailing conditions.

The lack of independent supervision was another matter. Every convention insisted that certain officials, unconnected with
either party, must be present to ensure fair play. Another point
was that, to prevent either participant tampering with the
weapons or otherwise obtaining an unfair advantage, the pistols
should belong to the officials and be brought to the dueling
ground in a locked and sealed box.

"Will twenty-five paces be acceptable?" Pierre-Quint asked
as he and Jaloux joined Ole Devil's seconds, leaving Dumoulin
standing disconsolately.

"It will," Hallistead confirmed, knowing that his principal
was an excellent pistol shot.

"The pistols are charged smooth and single," Pierre-Quint stated, offering both weapons butt-first to the entertainer. "We will allow your principal to make the first selection."

"We accept, with thanks," Hallistead answered formally, as such an assurance on the part of another gentleman was held to be sufficient proof that the weapons were identical in every respect, including the way they had been loaded. "Do you wish my principal to remove his shirt?"

"It won't be necessary," Pierre-Quint replied, although there was a sound reason why he should have said yes. "Shall I have mine take off his jacket?"

"There's no need," Hallistead said, knowing that to do so would offer Ole Devil no advantage. "Now, sir, what are your intentions with regard to our principals' firing positions?"

The question was in order. While the challenged party had the choice of weapons and venue, the challenger was entitled to select the distance between the firing of pistols. However, Pierre-Quint did not consult Dumoulin and made only a cursory study of their surroundings.

"It is of no consequence," the Creole remarked in an offhand manner. "The light is equally good over the whole area, and there isn't enough wind to affect the flight of the bullets."

"As you will," the entertainer acceded, and turned to Dumoulin's other second. "If you will pace off the required distance across the center, sir, Mr. Okasi can mark the firing positions."

Going to the side of the hollow, Jaloux watched the Oriental scuffing an X in the soil with the heel of his right boot. Then the young Creole stepped out twenty-five long paces, and where he stopped, Tommy marked the spot in the same manner.

"We should have a director of the duel, sir," Hallistead pointed out while the marking was taking place. "However, under the circumstances it is permissible for one of us to officiate."

"Will you do the honors, sir?" Pierre-Quint inquired, accepting that the entertainer's summation was correct and seeing that he could use it to serve his own purpose.

"I will," Hallistead agreed, and turned his attention to the principals. "Will you come and select your weapons, gentlemen? I am required to point out that it is *not* permissible to test the trigger pull by cocking and lowering the hammer."

Advancing, Dumoulin allowed Ole Devil to precede him and make the first choice. Having done so, the Texian watched the youngster take the remaining pistol. Noticing the slight hesitancy Dumoulin displayed while doing so, he decided that it was not because his own selection had spoiled an arrangement to gain an advantage through a discrepancy in the weapon's loads.

"You will now take your places on the marks," Hallistead continued after the pair had armed themselves. "When you are in position, I will say, 'Attention! *Feu!—Un!—Deux!—Trois!* at this speed. If either is not ready at the word *attention,* he may say so without prejudice. But otherwise, after the word *feu!* is given, he raises his pistol and must fire *before* the count reaches *trois.* Is that all understood and acceptable to both of you?"

"Perfectly," Ole Devil drawled instantly, and his whole attitude was redolent of complete confidence.

"Y—yes!" Dumoulin assented, after a brief pause, the word emerging like the pop of a tightly fitting cork being drawn from the neck of a bottle.

"Then, gentlemen," Hallistead said in tones of awesome finality, "take your places, please."

The pistol in Dumoulin's right hand seemed to weigh remarkably heavy as, knowing that the die was cast, he walked slowly to where Jaloux was waiting. With each step he felt his anxiety increasing. He realized that his pride and his companions' insistence had led him into a terribly perilous predicament. While he had been taught how to shoot, he was all too aware that he was anything but an expert marksman. Not, he told himself miserably, that he was any more skillful with a sword. Yet he could see no possible way of evading the duel now that the preparations had gone so far. Even to make an attempt would brand him forever as a coward.

Taking his place upon the mark, without meeting his second's eyes, Dumoulin stared across the hollow. Just over twenty-five yards away, the Texian was already in position. Still radiating self-assurance, as if certain of how the affair would turn out, he was handing his personal weapons to the Oriental. Determined to try to appear just as confident, the youngster passed his own pistol to Jaloux and refastened his jacket.

Again Dumoulin studied his adversary. If he had known more about such affairs, he would have realized that Pierre-Quint had put him at a disadvantage when discussing how the principals should dress. The Texian's buckskin shirt was far less distinguishable against the background of the hollow's bare sides than his own black coat and white shirt would be.

"Make ready, gentlemen," Hallistead called from where he —in his capacity as director of the duel—and Pierre-Quint were standing. They had positioned themselves midway between the adversaries and about six yards out of the line of fire. "Cock your pistols."

Drawing a deep breath, Dumoulin reached for and drew back his weapon's hammer. A more experienced man would have known that the soft click made by the operating mechanism signified a very light trigger pull. To the youngster the sound only meant that he was even closer to the terrifying climax. He silently promised himself that, providing he survived, he would never again be foolish enough to allow himself to be persuaded to become involved in another duel, especially one that every ounce of his being warned should never have, and need never have, happened.

Having made his resolution, the youngster forced himself to follow the procedure he had been taught was mandatory in such a situation. Turning sideways to the line of fire, he wondered if doing so really did present his adversary a more difficult target. His knowledge of anatomy, scanty as it was at that time, warned that there were considerations that outweighed the possible advantage. He made sure that he kept his right elbow pressed against his right hip, held the pistol's butt to his thigh and pointed its barrel downward.[2]

2. In a formal duel, if a participant moved the pistol into alignment before the word *feu,* or fired after the word *trois,* and, in either case, killed his

Noticing how his opponent was standing, Dumoulin's misgiving over his own posture increased. He also doubted that the Texian's hand was feeling as unsteady as his own. While Captain Hardin did not have a reputation as a duelist, he had already been involved in considerable fighting and was held in high esteem for his courage.

Although Ole Devil had never aspired to gain a name as a duelist, he had accepted that circumstances might compel him to engage in an "affair of honor." So he had concluded that the traditional sideways stance was not the most effective. The slight advantage in the reduction of the target area was overridden, in his opinion, by the fact that a wound received would prove more dangerous. A bullet that could perforate both lungs when sideways could only strike one if the recipient stood square to the shooter. Several other internal organs were also safer in the latter posture. By leaning forward slightly, which was permissible, the ribs were contracted and afforded protection to the heart and lungs. Finally one could take aim better when standing facing the object to be hit than one could when craning the head around to look over the right shoulder, which hampered the raised arm and strained the eyes.

Bearing those points in mind, the Texian stood with his feet astride the line; but kept his pistol as was prescribed.

"Attention!" Hallistead barked, then paused to see whether either participant wished to raise an objection.

To Dumoulin it seemed that time was standing still.

Staring at the tall, slender, and menacing figure, so near yet somehow so far away, he was filled with a sense of foreboding. The Texian's tanned face was so much like the portraits he had seen of the devil that it was even more unnerving. Only by exercising all his willpower did the youngster control his urge to throw down his weapon and run.

Satisfied that the duelists were ready, Hallistead continued with the ritual. Sometimes a director of the duel would hurry his count with the intention of confusing the adversaries and

---

man, he could be tried for murder should his adversary's seconds lodge a complaint over the infringement.—J.T.E.

lessening the chances of either fatally injuring the other by taking a long and careful aim. But the entertainer did not hurry. Instead, as he had warned when giving the instructions, he continued to speak at the speed—equivalent to one hundred words a minute—prescribed by convention.

"Feu!—Un!—Deux!—Trois!"

At the first word, acting on the signal to commence, Dumoulin and Ole Devil began to raise their right arms. Instantly the differences between their frame of mind and respective ability became obvious.

Where the Texian was elevating his pistol with a smoothly flowing motion, the youngster's weapon came up in an almost spasmodic jerk.

Before Dumoulin could take any kind of aim, in fact only chance was causing the barrel to point in Ole Devil's direction, his right forefinger twitched involuntarily. Slight as the gesture was, it proved sufficient to operate the light pull of the trigger. To his horror he saw the hammer begin to snap forward.

There was a sharp crack as the pistol's firing charge was detonated!

Gushing from the muzzle, the whitish gases of the burned powder obscured Dumoulin's target. In spite of that, his every instinct warned him that he could not have made a hit.

An instant later, as the cloud drifted away, the youngster found that his supposition was correct!

Dumoulin realized that nothing could save him from the Mephistophelian-featured Texian's response.

Nor was a man of Ole Devil Hardin's ability likely to miss!

No spurt of smoke and flame erupted from the muzzle of the Texian's pistol as a warning that a swiftly flying portion of lead had already been emitted.

Instead, showing not the slightest concern over having a bullet pass by very close to his head, Ole Devil continued to swing the pistol around until it was held behind his back.

"J'ai oublié!" the Texian announced, and repeated it in English, "I have forgotten."

For a moment Dumoulin was numbed by a mixture of amazement and relief. At first he could not appreciate what was happening. Then an understanding flooded through him. It was followed by a feeling of gratitude toward his adversary. By acting in such a manner, Captain Hardin was offering a way by which the duel could be brought to an end without the need for any further exchange of shots. What was more, the youngster knew that he could now withdraw with honor.

In the hope of preventing frivolous and trivial challenges and to make opponents realize that a duel was a matter of life and death, every convention, and the Clonmel Code in particular, prohibited deliberately firing to miss an adversary.[3] It did happen, of course, but there was a more dignified and honorable means if one had no desire to injure one's opponent. By placing the pistol behind the back and declaring, *"J'ai oublié,"* the duelist displayed his intentions in a manner that left no doubt as to their interpretation.

"Wh—!" Pierre-Quint gasped, watching Ole Devil hand the discharged pistol to Tommy Okasi and retrieve his own weapons. "What—?"

"Shots have been exchanged," Hallistead answered, and there was just a hint of relief in his voice. "Honor is now satisfied, and the affair is over."

"Over?" the Creole yelped, but the entertainer was already walking away. So, scowling furiously, he strode toward Dumoulin and Jaloux.

By the time Hallistead joined his companions, Ole Devil had sheathed the bowie knife and was returning the pistol to its loop on the belt.

"You handled that with the kind of foresight and acumen that I expected of you, if I may so say, sir," the entertainer said in praise. "However, the *gentlemen* from New Orleans may not be in concurrence."

3. Clonmel Code, Commandment 12: No dumb firing, or firing in the air, is admissable in any case. The challenger ought not to have challenged without receiving offense, and the challenged, if he gave offense, ought to have made an apology before he came to the ground; therefore children's play must be dishonorable on one side or the other and is accordingly prohibited.—J.T.E.

"They'd better be," Ole Devil growled, glancing to where the Creoles were talking, gesticulating to their principal. "I'm in no mood to go on with this damned farce."

"Could I suggest we make it appear that we are taking our departure?" Hallistead asked. "That should provoke them into declaring their intentions."

"Let's do that," Ole Devil agreed, and the entertainer felt he would rather not be in the other party's shoes if they did raise any objections.

"Hey there!" Pierre-Quint shouted, seeing the three men turning as if meaning to leave the hollow. Stalking forward with Jaloux at his side, they were followed by Dumoulin, who was still carrying the empty pistol. "We haven't finished yet. There must be another shot."

"Like hell there must!" said Ole Devil, spinning around and stepping away from his companions. Such was the concentrated venom in his voice as he confronted the approaching trio that they came to a halt. "It's over! Finished! *Done!*"

"That isn't for you to say," Jaloux protested. "Your seconds—!"

"Listen to me, damn you!" the Texian commanded, his face as malevolent as that of his namesake when condemning a sinner to eternal torment. Glancing past the two older Creoles, he continued in a more gentle fashion. "What I'm going to say doesn't include you, M'sieur Dumoulin. You have conducted yourself with courage and credit throughout this whole unfortunate affair. I trust that you will agree that our difficulties have been settled honorably and we no longer have any quarrel?"

"I do, sir," the youngster affirmed, showing a greater enthusiasm than had been in evidence up to that point.

"You can't—!" Pierre-Quint began, looking around.

"The hell he can't!" Ole Devil put in, bringing the Creole's attention back to him. "I've played along with your damned charade as far as I intend to. We're engaged in a war with a bloodthirsty, malevolent tyrant and have neither the time nor the need for dissension in our ranks. So I'm warning you that the next man who comes to challenge me, whether it is one of you six or your regiment's *fencing master,* he'd better be holding a weapon, because I'll kill him where he stands without bothering with any formalities."

Nobody listening to the quietly spoken yet impassioned words could doubt that the speaker meant exactly what he said. However, Pierre-Quint and Jaloux had an added reason to take notice of the statement. They realized from the way in which the Texian emphasized his reference to their regiment's fencing master that he had something specific in mind, and they drew the correct conclusions over what it might be.

"He knows, Marcel!" Jaloux screeched, reaching for Dumoulin's pistol which he had pushed into his belt when it was handed to him. "Defend yourself!" [4]

4. The author realizes that the procedure for a duel with pistols in this chapter differs from that described in the "The Futility of War" episode of *The Fastest Gun in Texas.* However, he wishes to point out that duelists in the United States of America occasionally adopted methods that did not conform to the European conventions.—J.T.E.

6

HE'S LUCKY TO BE ALIVE

Standing slightly to one side and behind Ole Devil Hardin, Tommy Okasi realized that something must be done—and quickly—to bring an end to Lieutenant Gérard Jaloux's ill-advised behavior before he paid a high price for his folly. The Oriental also considered that he was the member of his party best suited to bring this about. As their acquaintance had only been brief, he did not know whether Mangrove Hallistead was capable of handling the situation. However, one thing of which he was certain was that his employer was not at that moment in a mood to suffer fools gladly and might respond in a regrettable manner. So Tommy decided to act on his own initiative. Regardless of his small size, he was eminently qualified to do so.

Although Jaloux and Lieutenant Marcel Pierre-Quint had pretended to accept that Tommy was socially eligible as the Texian's second in the duel, the acquiescence had been to serve their personal purposes. Neither of them had believed the entertainer's explanation about the Oriental's status as a member of the Japanese lower nobility—which was perfectly true—or that he was a competent warrior in his own right.

The Creoles were to be given a *very* convincing proof of the latter point!

One of the samurai's most remarkable and impressive martial accomplishments was *laijitsu,* the swift withdrawal of the *daisho*'s longer, *tachi* sword.[1] With the possible exception of an ancient Roman legionary's ability to pull out his *gladius,* it was a feat unequaled by the swordsmen of the Western Hemisphere. In fact, similar heights of rapidity would only be attained when, during the late 1860s, the gunfighters of the Old West began to experiment with the possibilities of drawing and shooting a revolver—which was not much longer than the hilt of a *tachi*—at speed.[2] Nor would such methods achieve their full potential until the arrival of techniques developed by twentieth-century combat shooting experts, who employed even more compact weapons and sophisticated equipment.[3]

Certainly there was nothing in Texas, or the United States for that matter, in the 1830s that might have served as a warning to Jaloux and Pierre-Quint of what was to come.

Bounding past Ole Devil and Hallistead, giving neither of them an opportunity to take any action, the little Oriental sent his right hand flashing to the hilt of the *tachi.* Before he alighted in front of the two young dandies, brief as the movement had been, he had already slid the thirty-inch-long blade from its sheath. Still moving with the same remarkable speed, giving the spiritual cry of *"Kiai!"* he swung the naked weapon in a smooth and graceful arc toward Jaloux.

Before the amazed Creole could even grasp the butt of the pistol, much less pluck it from his belt, he saw the shining and obviously exceptionally sharp blade approaching as if his right arm was a magnet attracting the steel. Instinctively, if involuntarily, he snatched the threatened limb clear of the danger.

1. New readers can find further details about Tommy Okasi's *daisho,* or matched pair of swords, in Appendix B.—J.T.E.
2. Information about the methods of the Old West's gunfighters is given in the author's "Floating Outfit," "Waco," "Calamity Jane," "Brady Anchor and Jefferson Trade," "John Slaughter," and "Waxahachie Smith" series.—J.T.E.
3. Details of various combat-shooting techniques and equipment can be found in the author's Rockabye County "Modern Western Law Enforcement" series.—J.T.E.

Having prevented Jaloux from drawing the weapon, Tommy treated him, Pierre-Quint, Hallistead, and Lieutenant Alphonse Jules Dumoulin to a masterful exhibition of sword handling in the Japanese fashion. He also drove all thoughts of further aggression from Jaloux's and Pierre-Quint's minds. Even Ole Devil, who had frequently watched the Oriental practicing with the *tachi,* was impressed with the display.

Around and around, back and forth, up and down darted the long and—to Occidental eyes—strangely shaped sword. For all its relatively cumbersome appearance, Tommy made thrusts or cuts with the facility of an *épée-de-combat,* or saber, but without making contact with either of the startled young Creoles. Although neither was as much as scratched in passing, each was all too aware of just how slender a margin they were being missed by. Fortunately for them, surprise at the transformation of one whom they had previously dismissed as no more than a harmless servant froze them into immobility.

Sometimes the *tachi* was held in one hand, then it would be grasped in both. Either way, nothing interfered with the rapid, flowing motions of the razor-sharp blade that had a pliancy and strength all but unequaled in the Western Hemisphere. As the weapon moved, almost of its own volition, Tommy heightened the effect by bobbing, weaving, advancing and retreating, but always judging his distance to a fraction of an inch to avoid injuring the now thoroughly alarmed and frightened young men.

For a good two minutes, although it seemed far longer to the Creoles and the onlookers, the Oriental kept up the demonstration. Then, giving another yell, he pivoted around. On returning to face the pair, he cut left and upward, then back at a downward angle to the right in quick succession. A sliver of material was sliced from the crown of Jaloux's "planter's" hat, without it being knocked from his head. A moment later, its knot severed, the sling that had supported Pierre-Quint's dislocated right shoulder fell away. Gasps of amazement burst from the watchers as Tommy returned the *tachi* to its sheath as swiftly as he had removed it.

None of the party in the hollow moved or spoke for several

seconds. In fact Jaloux and Pierre-Quint were incapable of speech or movement.

Even as Hallistead was about to make a comment, the silence was broken from another direction.

Footsteps sounded, drawing the group's attention to two people who were coming in some haste down the slope. In the lead, his face even more florid than it usually was, strode the commanding officer of the New Orleans Wildcats. Colonel Jules Dumoulin was followed by a small, dainty, very shapely, and beautiful blond-haired woman. Her poise and carriage lent a somewhat seductive grace to what, on a person less well favored, would have been a plain and serviceable black riding habit. Her expressive features were registering a mixture of concern and alarm.

"I heard a shot!" the colonel bellowed, coming to a smart military halt a few feet from the other men, and went on to ask a purely rhetorical question. "What's been happening here?"

"It began as an affair of honor," Hallistead replied, showing neither surprise at the newcomers' arrival nor concern over Dumoulin's obvious disapproval. He threw a pointed look at the still-rigid and pallid-faced Jaloux and Pierre-Quint, each of whom was now very ill at ease. Then he continued. "Unfortunately, Colonel, there are those who appear to have a strange conception of what such an affair entails, or when it should be considered at an end."

"An affair of honor?" Dumoulin repeated, as if such an idea had never entered his head. Then he glared at each of his subordinates in succession and with a scowl that his nephew, for one, sensed boded no good for them. However, instead of addressing any of the trio, he swung his gaze elsewhere and demanded harshly, "Is it usual in Texas to engage a man who is partially incapacitated, Captain Hardin?"

Despite the question, Dumoulin did not really believe the young Texian would have agreed to fight a duel with either of the injured pair. In fact, from what he had seen of Ole Devil during the interview in Major General Samuel Houston's tent, he was surprised that such an affair had happened. However, he had asked in the hope that his own men would do the honorable thing by correcting his apparently erroneous and unjustified conclusion.

"It was against your nephew, who is totally capacitated, that Captain Hardin was engaged, Colonel," Hallistead put in, before the young man in question could do as his uncle desired. "These *gentlemen* were his seconds."

Although annoyed by the interruption, as he had sensed that his nephew was going to make the explanation, Dumoulin decided to restrain his inclination to turn his wrath upon the speaker. Nobody could say exactly what rank, if any, Hallistead held in the Republic of Texas's Army,[4] but it was common knowledge that he stood very high in the commanding general's favor.

It was an awareness of Hallistead's standing with Houston that had made the colonel accompany his wife, Corrinne, to the site of the duel. She had told him that some of his young officers were at the Grand Hotel and, in spite of his orders, were expressing their intention of seeking out Ole Devil Hardin and delivering a challenge to a duel. Arriving at the hotel, they had learned that the confrontation had already taken place and that the participants had set out for the confrontation. So they had followed in the hope that Dumoulin would be in time to intervene.

Hearing the shot, the colonel had known he was too late to prevent the duel. However, on reaching the top of the hollow, he had discovered with relief that nobody was hurt. He still wanted to get to the bottom of the matter and find out why his orders had been disobeyed. In addition, there were other puzzling aspects that he wished to solve.

"Did you exchange shots with my nephew, Captain Hardin?" Dumoulin inquired, but in a considerably more polite tone.

"Only *I* fired, sir," Alphonse Dumoulin declared, giving the Texian no chance or need to speak for himself. "Captain Hardin said, *'J'ai oublé.'*"

---

4. Ole Devil Hardin had addressed Mangrove Hallistead as "captain" to make it acceptable for the entertainer to act as one of his seconds.—J.T.E.

"Very well!" the colonel barked, eyeing the three now clearly worried young men malevolently. "Return to our lines immediately and without speaking to *anybody*. Consider yourselves under arrest. I'll attend to you when I come back."

"May I say that Captain Hardin isn't at fault, sir?" young Dumoulin requested, standing fast while Jaloux and Pierre-Quint, the latter supporting his injured limb with his other hand, were almost scuttling from the hollow. On reaching the top, they stared ahead, then swung off at an acute angle. "The challenge was on my part, and he behaved in a gentlemanly fashion throughout."

"I never thought it was otherwise," the colonel replied, with just a hint of softening in his stern attitude. "Now get going, damn you!"

"Further to what the young man said, Colonel," Hallistead remarked as Alphonse Dumoulin followed his departing companions. "He's lucky to be alive. Not every man in Captain Hardin's position would have shown a similar restraint."

"Your *officer*'s behavior was misguided, but exemplary, sir," Ole Devil elaborated. "I didn't consider that the matter called for the shedding of blood."

"My thanks for your forbearance, sir," Dumoulin answered, noticing how the Texian had not alluded to his relationship with the youngster. "Alphonse owes you his life.[5] The hotheaded and prideful young fool—" He paused and stared up the slope in the direction taken by the errant trio and shook his head in puzzlement. "Yet he would have been the last I'd have expected to become involved in something like this. It's not as if he's like most of them, brought up to believe that the *code duello* is man's primary reason for existing. Just the opposite in fact. What's more, now I come to think of it, he's never been close friends, or even mixed much with any of that crowd."

"But he does have the advantage of being *your* nephew, Colonel," Hallistead pointed out.

"And what does *that* mean?" Dumoulin demanded.

5. How Alphonse Jules Dumoulin repaid the debt to Ole Devil Hardin is told in *Doc Leroy, M.D.*—J.T.E.

"I'm afraid that this whole affair cuts deeper than your nephew's hotheaded pride and misguided loyalty to the honor of your regiment," the entertainer warned. "In fact, at the risk of appending my nasal extremity where it has no right of entrance, I would suggest that you avail yourself of some reason to be rid of those two young fools before they cause some catastrophe in the regiment."

"*Two* young fools?" Dumoulin queried.

"You may also have to send your nephew home, to avoid any suggestion of favoritism," Hallistead admitted. "But his companions should go. They were willing to throw away his life as a means of extracting a spiteful vengeance upon Captain Hardin—"

"I thought they'd got him into it!" Dumoulin growled.

"They did," Hallistead confirmed. "Nor, even if they had given a thought to the consequences, which is doubtful, did they care how the success of their nefarious—nay, infamous—scheme could cause grave dissension, perhaps worse, in the rest of the Republic of Texas's Army."

"I'd like an explanation—!" Dumoulin stated, eyeing the entertainer grimly.

"Manny dear," Corrinne remarked, her voice suggesting that it, too, had been trained to reach the back row of a large theater in the days when there were no acoustical aids to make this possible. She threw a pointed glance out of the hollow. "All this is *very* interesting, and obviously, the colonel is eager to hear more, but wouldn't it be advisable for us to find somewhere less —open—to continue the discussion?"

"As ever, my dove, you are showing inestimable wisdom," Hallistead replied with a bow, employing the flamboyantly gallant manner in which he always addressed his wife. Having heard certain significiant sounds beyond the rim, he guessed what had prompted her comment. "While I realize that you have many duties demanding your attention, Colonel, may I suggest that you accompany us at least as far as the Grand Hotel and I will give you an explanation on the way."

"I will," Dumoulin assented. "From what you've said so far,

the sooner I get to the bottom of this affair, the better for all concerned."

"Tommy," Ole Devil drawled as the party was walking toward the slope. "Go and tell Colonel Fog, with my compliments, what's happened and ask him if he'll place the town off limits to all members of the Texas Light Cavalry until noon tomorrow."

"Smart thinking, Captain," Dumoulin said in praise, as the Oriental hurried away. "I'll make sure that none of my men come into San Felipe before we march for Harrisburg in the morning. Let's hope this business is all forgotten and that we can get along with each other better when the rest of the army joins us there."

"Yes, sir," Ole Devil replied, although he knew that if the assignment he was being sent on was a success, everybody was likely to have too much to occupy them to worry about petty differences.

"And now, sir," the colonel said, with an air of impatience, looking at Hallistead. "What have you to tell me?"

"Reprehensible as the practice is," the entertainer began grandiloquently, "there are times when eavesdropping upon a private conversation is not only excusable, but mandatory. Such an occasion was presented to me earlier this afternoon when, driven by the irresistible urgings of my bodily functions, I was compelled to hie myself to the hotel's toilet. While sitting within, I heard the two young men—"

At that moment, having ascended from the hollow as he was speaking, Hallistead's explanation was brought to an end. Ahead of his party, some distance away, stood a good-sized group of men. They had been gathering in much the same place when Corrinne had brought Dumoulin, and their excited chatter had caused her to make her suggestion about departing. Much to his relief, Ole Devil noticed that they all appeared to be Texians and that there were no obvious members of the New Orleans Volunteers present. His misgivings and sentiments on the latter point were soon proved to be justified.

"What's been coming off down there, Cap'n Hardin?" called one of the crowd as the Texian and his companions approached them. "Did you-all have to hand one of them high-faluting dudes from New Orleans his needings?"

"Way they've been taking on airs since they got here," another of the assembly continued, "it's sure enough time somebody did."

From the rumble of concurrence that arose, the speaker had expressed the feelings of all those around him.

A surge of anger rose within Ole Devil as he listened to the comments, and a low snort of indignation burst from Dumoulin. Having just endangered his life by taking a calculated risk to avert further dissension in the ranks of the Republic of Texas's Army, he was in no mood to see his efforts brought to nothing by the behavior of men who had little to keep them occupied and so were ripe for mischief.

Despite having been all too aware of the hostility that already existed between the Texians and the Creoles, Ole Devil had realized that there was no way he could avoid fighting the duel. Alphonse Dumoulin's pride had been so aroused by his companions that no kind of refusal would have ended the matter. In fact the Texian had sensed that the youngster would have gone as far as striking him as an added inducement if all else had failed.

Studying Dumoulin's nervous attitude and attempts to delay the proceedings, Ole Devil had been confident that he could terminate the affair without bloodshed provided it was not aggravated. However, if he had been struck, such leniency would have been out of the question. So he had agreed to the duel, gambling that the youngster's perturbation was detrimental to accuracy. Nor, even after Hallistead had told him about the scheme hatched by Jaloux and Pierre-Quint, had he changed his mind about his line of action.

Incensed by their treatment at Ole Devil's hands and guessing what had caused it, the two young Creoles had been determined that they would take their revenge in spite of their superior's comments on the matter. Nor had they expected any difficulty in obtaining help. Feelings were running high over the orders to leave in the morning for Harrisburg, and could be turned to their advantage.

First the pair had spoken with their regiment's fencing master. He was a noted duelist and generally ready to demonstrate his "courage" on the "field of honor." However, when they had told him of their wishes, he had said he would be willing to represent them had it not been for Colonel Dumoulin's orders. Refusing to be thwarted, they had sought for another substitute.

Finding a similar reluctance to disobey the commanding officer among the more likely potential candidates, Jaloux and Pierre-Quint had concluded they must try some other means. They had selected Alphonse Dumoulin, knowing he was unlikely to survive a duel with such a capable fighting man as Ole Devil had proved to be because he was the colonel's nephew. They had felt sure that, on hearing that he had been killed or wounded by the Texian, his uncle would withdraw the prohibition and so free the fencing master to uphold the "honor" of the New Orleans Wildcats.

Unfortunately for the pair, they had been discussing the fencing master's reluctance and how they planned to overcome it while they, but not Dumoulin, were making use of the hotel's toilet. Little knowing that they were being overheard, they had said enough for Hallistead to deduce what was afoot and appreciate its implications. Sending his wife to inform Colonel Dumoulin, in the hope that he would arrive quickly enough to make an official intervention, the entertainer had intended to find and warn Ole Devil. However, he had been delayed by meeting a man who had something of importance to tell him. By the time they had concluded their business, the confrontation was already taking place.

Guessing what the Texian had in mind, Hallistead had also duplicated the summation with regard to Dumoulin's unsuitability for participation. So he had been willing to render his assistance. Appreciating the advisability of keeping the affair restricted to as few people as possible, he had used some information he had been given by Ole Devil during their first meeting as a means of persuading the Creoles to accept Tommy in the capacity of second, thus helping to hurry the proceedings along.

Having achieved his purpose by bringing the duel to a blood-less conclusion and allowing Dumoulin to emerge with honor, Ole Devil was now faced with an extension of the problem created by the Creoles' scheme. He had known that they could not hope to keep the affair a secret, but counted upon it not arousing too much attention. As it had, he knew that he must prevent it from being exploited by his fellow Texians as an excuse for displaying dislike and resentment of their allies from the United States.

Looking around the crowd, he recognized only a few of them and could count upon just two as friends. None of them were members of the Texas Light Cavalry. So he realized that he could not rely upon his rank, or military authority, to disperse them. Instead he would have to employ the strength of his personality and try to subjugate them to his will. If he could, he might cause the affair to blow over—unless the angry Colonel Dumoulin said or did something to spoil his chances.

Let *that* happen, the young Texian told himself, and the New Orleans Wildcats could not depart quickly enough to avoid further clashes.

7

WE'RE FIGHTING A WAR

"I thank you for taking such an interest, gentlemen," said Ole Devil Hardin in a tone that held no suggestion that the gratitude was genuine. Striding ahead of his companions, he hoped Colonel Jules Dumoulin would have the good sense to keep quiet. "But it was a *private* matter and has been settled with honor and to the satisfaction of both sides."

"Oh dear!" Corrinne Hallistead exclaimed, stopping and waggling her right foot as the Texian spoke and increased his pace. "I seem to have a stone in my shoe. Could you lend me your arm for a moment, Colonel?"

"Certainly, madame," the burly Creole replied, guessing what the Texian was trying to do and not being averse to having an excuse to let him get on with it. Coming to a halt, he allowed the little blonde to brace herself against his arm. "Will you have to take the shoe off?"

"I think not," Corrinne decided after a moment. She watched what was happening.

"Did you—?" a member of the crowd began, as the blonde made her request for help.

"As I said," Ole Devil interrupted, conscious that he was moving forward alone and pleased by Corrinne's intervention.

The cold glare he directed at the speaker did as much as his chillingly prohibitive words to prevent the question from being completed. His hard eyes raked the rest of the assembly as he went on quietly, but with deadly emphasis. "And I'd be obliged if I don't have to *repeat* it. The affair was *private,* and I wouldn't thank *anybody* who wasn't involved for expressing an interest in it."

There the suddenly quiet and attentive crowd had it!

The situation had been laid out as plainly as even the least discerning of them could desire!

Looking at the straight-backed young Texian standing before them, feet apart and thumbs tucked close to the weapons on his waist belt, every member of the crowd deduced that he would not countenance any further questions. What was more, they could tell he had every intention of enforcing his wishes. Knowing his well-deserved reputation for being a "lil ole devil for a fight," they did not doubt he was capable of doing it if the need should arise.

Everything, as Ole Devil was painfully aware, depended upon what happened next. From his examination he felt sure that none of the crowd had had enough to drink to induce a frame of mind where *any* challenge must be taken up. For all that, somebody might feel it incumbent upon himself to do so.

"By cracky, though, the cap'n's right," declared one of the scouts who had been with "Deaf" Smith at the Grand Hotel that afternoon and who now stood in the forefront of the crowd. "Seeing's everything's been settled fair 'n' square, it ain't *nobody* else's never-mind."

"Way it strikes me," the second of the aged chief of scouts' companions continued, from another part of the assembly. "What went on 'tween you-all 'n' those other young fellers's your own doings, Cap'n. Which it ain't the way of us Texians, no matter what folks does 'otherwhere,' to go poking our noses into other folks's personal 'n' private doings. That's what we're set to fight Santa Anna over."

Studying the crowd's reactions to the two comments, Ole Devil could see they were producing a desirable effect. Of course the identities of the men who had made them were help-

ing. "Deaf" Smith and his small force of scouts were respected
and admired by the majority of Texians, having been in the
forefront all through the conflict. It had fallen upon them to
investigate the rumors that the Alamo Mission had been taken.
Given three days to complete the task, they had returned the
following evening escorting the wife of Captain Almeron Dick-
inson—who, with her young daughter, had been present all
through the siege—after her release by Santa Anna. What was
more, the reference to the Texians' trait of minding their own
business could not be overlooked; particularly with one of the
despised Louisianans in the vicinity.

Showing no sign of his feelings, but counting upon the people
with him to act correctly, Ole Devil started to walk slowly
forward. Having drawn similar conclusions, Mangrove Hallistead stepped out to catch up with him. Smiling her thanks at
Dumoulin, Corrinne put off the pretense of shaking the stone
from beneath her foot and followed. By the time the Texian was
almost on the crowd, his companions had joined him. No more
questions were asked, and the onlookers parted to let his party
through.

"Whew!" Hallistead exclaimed, sotto voce once they were
beyond the crowd. "You really told them, my Mephistophelian
young friend. Let us hope that they bear in mind what you said
and allow the incident to be forgotten."

"It's a pity they can't all be kept occupied by something to
make them forget it," Corrinne declared, frowning pensively.

"I doubt if anything short of the threat of an attack by the
Mexicans would do that, my dear," Hallistead replied. "And
I'm afraid such a contingency is remote."

"That's true, madame," Dumoulin went on. "According to
our scouts, there aren't any Mexicans within miles."

"Good heavens!" Corrinne gasped, looking very concerned.
"Does that mean nobody is keeping watch for them?"

Remembering their last meeting,[1] Ole Devil was puzzled by
the woman's attitude. Demure, petite, and fragile though she
might appear, he had had no cause to think of her as the fright-

1. Described in *Ole Devil and the Mule Train.*—J.T.E.

ened and helpless female she seemed to be at that moment.
Glancing at her husband in the hope of enlightenment, he
failed to detect a clue on a face that—like the woman's—was
capable of producing whatever kind of expression or emotion
the situation called for.

"They are, madame, never fear," Dumoulin said, clearly
having none of the Texian's misgivings. Instead all his masculine protective instincts were aroused by the little blonde's apparent perturbation, and he wanted to reassure her. "Some of
Colonel Smith's scouts are always on watch well to our rear.
There's no chance of the Mexicans arriving without our knowing."

"Oh, that *is* a relief!" Corrinne said with a sigh and, looking
a little less worried, continued, "Manny darling, don't you
think you should tell the colonel about the cause of the
duel?"

"Egad yes, my dove, I do and I will," the entertainer agreed,
and started to comply with something less than his usual ver-
bosity.

Before Dumoulin had heard the whole of what lieutenants
Gérard Jaloux and Marcel Pierre-Quint had tried to bring
about, a splutter of explosive French profanity erupted from
him. Then, remembering that there was a lady present—although Corrinne was showing neither distress nor horror at the
vehemence of his reaction—he made a visible effort to control
his temper and listened to the rest of the explanation in silent,
ever-growing anger.

"The damned young fools!" the colonel spat out after Hallistead had stopped speaking. "Did *Maître d'armes* de Lepage
know what they were up to?"

"They didn't say he did in so many words," the entertainer
admitted. "But I received the impression that he was not averse
to the possibility of being able to engage Captain Hardin in a
duel. Is he the kind of man who would countenance such an
irresponsible scheme?"

"He's acquired a name as a duelist as well as a fencing master," Dumoulin replied. "Men of that kind generally want to

enhance their reputations by taking to the 'field of honor,' particularly against somebody who is regarded as being a capable fighting man himself. But I don't want to say he would have agreed to the scheme if he'd been told about it."

"Is he likely to take up for those two, sir?" Ole Devil inquired.

"He knows my orders on the matter," the colonel said. "He also knows that he's anything but my *beau idéal* for a *maître d'armes*. So I think that *he'll* think twice, as he did when they asked him in the first place, before he does anything to give me an excuse to get rid of him."

"May I make a request, sir?" Ole Devil asked, his tone formally respectful.

"You may, Captain," Dumoulin authorized.

"Will you ensure that all your men know I have taken part in my *last* duel?" the Texian said. "We're fighting a war against the Mexicans, not with each other. So I'll consider the next man who issues a challenge to be an enemy and treat him accordingly."

"I understand and concur, Captain," Dumoulin declared, impressed by the complete lack of bombast or arrogance in the young man's attitude. He was doing no more than stating a fact that he had every intention of putting into effect. "And I'd like to thank you again on my nephew's behalf. Now, if you'll excuse me, I have my duties to attend to. I'll do everything in my power to prevent any further mischief."

"I wouldn't like to be in those three's shoes when he gets back," Ole Devil remarked, watching the colonel stamping away.

"He's in a somewhat difficult position, for all of that," Hallistead pointed out. "Being in command of a privately financed volunteer regiment puts a serious limit to the extent of his disciplinary powers, as you may have cause to know."

"It does, although we're luckier than most in that respect," Ole Devil answered. "But I hope that he can keep them under control until we leave. I meant what I told him."

"He didn't doubt it," the entertainer declared. "And I'm

certain he'll find a way to make sure they don't cause trouble in the future."[2]

"By the way," Ole Devil said. "I was coming to see you when I met them. Can you spare me a few minutes, please?"

"Certainly," Hallistead affirmed. "The Grand Hotel is in the offing. Shall we avail ourselves of its far from extensive facilities?"

"I'd rather be getting back to my company, if it's all the same with you," Ole Devil objected. "Fooling with them's kept me away much longer than I intended, and I still have a lot to do to get ready for the morning."

"That's understandable," Hallistead declared, knowing that Company C was leaving. "So I will perambulate thence with you and can pay my respects to Colonel Fog in passing. And what about you, light of my life?"

"I don't think I'll come," Corrinne replied. "Unless of course you need my advice, too, Captain Hardin?"

"While I'd count it an honor to be seen in your company, ma'am," the Texian replied, sweeping his hat off with a flourish, "your husband can tell me all I want to know."

"Then I'll go and wait for you at the hotel, darling," Corrinne informed her husband, glancing in that direction. "Why, there's charming Colonel Smith. I wonder if he's heard that there are any marauding bands of Mexicans in the vicinity. Perhaps he'll be able to put my mind at ease about it."

"I've heard 'Deaf' Smith called a whole heap of things, mostly deserved, on occasion," Ole Devil remarked, watching

2. Mangrove Hallistead's summation proved correct. Telling lieutenants Jaloux and Pierre-Quint that he knew of their intentions, Colonel Dumoulin gave them the choice of being sent back to Louisiana in disgrace or accompanying *Maître d'armes* de Lepage there on a "recruiting campaign." Having grown disenchanted with Texas and deciding it offered no profit for him, the fencing master accepted the assignment when it was presented to him. So did the other four who had been involved in the incident, and they also took their departure. Alphonse Dumoulin was dispatched, in a different party, ostensibly to purchase and arrange the delivery of medical supplies.—J.T.E.

the woman join the obviously delighted old chief of scouts, "but *charming* wasn't one of them."

"Or me, I admit," Hallistead replied.

"What do you think your lady's up to?" the Texian inquired.

"She *seems* deeply disturbed by the possibility that we will hear the Mexicans are approaching with the intention of launching an offensive," the entertainer suggested. "What would happen, do you think, if such a threat should eventuate?"

"Everybody would be too busy watching out for them to go around looking for mischief," Ole Devil surmised with a grin. "But it won't happen, *will it?*"

"As I told Corrinne, the contingency is remote," Hallistead answered, but his tone lacked conviction. They started to walk toward where the Texas Light Cavalry were camped, and he went on, "Now, in what manner do you wish me to render assistance?"

"I'm not at liberty to explain why," Ole Devil warned, "but I have to take a small party into the center of the Mexican Army."

"No easy task," Hallistead said quietly, showing no surprise. "How did you propose to accomplish it?"

"Would it be possible to disguise Tommy, the other man, and myself so we could get in there and carry out our assignment?"

"By day or at night?"

"We could move in to the center by night, but getting there and doing what we have to will mean working in daylight."

"Do you wish to impersonate specific people?" Hallistead asked, but his voice expressed no enthusiasm.

"No," Ole Devil replied. "Just to pass for Mexicans to avoid suspicion if we meet any. Once we've done our work, it doesn't matter if they realize we're Texians."

"To pass at a distance, you would require the appropriate garments and even saddles, which would be easy enough to obtain," Hallistead decided, being an authority on the subject of makeup and disguise since they had been his specialty in the theater. "However, at under fifty yards and with your face shaved and hair either hidden or cut, your features would prob-

ably give you away. That would be even more so in the case of
your worthy Oriental factotum. He could *never* pass as a person
of Latin origin. An Indian, maybe, with stain on his skin and
wearing a black wig, which I could supply."

"We don't intend to let anybody get *that* close on the way
in," Ole Devil pointed out. "And we can cover the final stage
during the night."

"True, but even in the darkness there could be problems.
Unless I'm prying beyond acceptable depths, is the third member of your party a Chicano?"

"A Texian."

"Then you will have the language problem to contend with
should you be challenged," the entertainer warned. "There are
sure to be sentries posted, and no matter how well you speak
Spanish, your accents might give you away."

"So you don't think much of our chances?"

"Not at close quarters," Hallistead admitted. "A disguise is
never entirely satisfactory, nor long lasting, when it requires
makeup and is for use outdoors. That would be particularly so
in the current inclement weather. It would require frequent
renewal, and that is no task to be undertaken without training.
No, my Mephistophelian young friend, there is no way you can
utilize a disguise at close quarters and be sure of success."

"That's just about what I figured," Ole Devil admitted, and
gave a shrug. "We'll just have to try it some other way."

"If you haven't completed the selection of your party, or
even if you have and consider the idea meritorious, I could
accompany you and renew the makeup when necessary," Hallistead offered. "Not even that will guarantee success, but it is
worthy of consideration."

"Thank you for the offer, sir," Ole Devil drawled. "But three
is the maximum that we could hope to take through."

"I'll leave that in your hands, Captain," the entertainer declared. "And I'm sorry I couldn't be of more help."

"You only closed up a way I wasn't really counting on, sir,"
Ole Devil drawled philosophically. "There's another open to
us. While I was on my way to collect the general's caplocks, I

picked up a letter of identification Santa Anna had given to a white renegade.[3] That might get us through."

"I hope that it does," Hallistead said sincerely, without attempting to try to find out the nature of the assignment. "Isn't this your second-in-command coming?"

"Yes," Ole Devil affirmed, looking to where Mannen Blaze was exhibiting an uncharacteristic haste as he strode toward them from the Texas Light Cavalry's neat lines of tents.

"In considerable haste too," the entertainer went on, frowning. "I hope that nothing is amiss."

"So do I," Ole Devil seconded grimly.

"Howdy, Mr. Hallistead," Mannen greeted, then gave his full attention to his superior. "Paul Dimmock's just come back, Cousin Devil."

"He made good time," Ole Devil said quietly, feeling sure that the redhead had something more to add.

"Sergeant Smith met them bringing in a herd of cattle they'd found," Mannen continued. "Trouble is, so did some fellers who heard about the fuss at the hotel. Paul told me he'd like to see you as soon as it's convenient."

"Where is he now?" Ole Devil asked, sensing his cousin had left much unsaid.

"Down at the horse lines, the last I saw of him," Mannen replied.

"I'll go and see him," Ole Devil decided. "If you'll excuse me, Mr. Hallistead?"

"Of course," the entertainer answered. "Is Colonel Fog available, Mr. Blaze?"

"Yes, sir," Mannen confirmed.

"Take Mr. Hallistead to see the colonel," Ole Devil ordered, and even though Mannen Blaze knew why Lieutenant Paul Dimmock had insisted upon the interview, he signified his assent without a moment's hesitation.

Leaving the burly redhead to escort the entertainer, Ole Devil walked swiftly through the camp. Making his way to the well-guarded lines of picketed horses, he was pleased to observe

3. Told in *Young Ole Devil.*—J.T.E.

that the man he was seeking stood alone and some distance
from the nearest sentry.

Since the destruction of his former regiment, along with the
other prisoners at Goliad, Paul Dimmock had laid aside the
attire of the New Orleans Grays and wore the uniform of an
officer in the Texas Light Cavalry. Almost as tall as Ole Devil,
he was slightly heavier in build and had short-cropped light-
brown hair. The bitter lines on his good-looking face had not
been there before the massacre of Colonel James Walker Fannin's command. Seeing his superior coming, he strode forward
with a demeanor of indignation and anger.

"Before you say what you're thinking," Ole Devil drawled as
they halted face-to-face, in his voice a coldly prohibitive note,
"don't!"

"You—!" Dimmock began, ignoring the warning.

"I took steps to prevent something stupidly senseless from
happening," Ole Devil interrupted. "You don't need to prove
anything, especially to a bunch of young fools with too much
time and not enough work on their hands."

"But they—!" Dimmock tried to protest.

"What would it have proved to call one, or all of them out?"
Ole Devil continued relentlessly. "Not a solitary damned thing,
and it would have settled less."

"It would have proved that—" Dimmock tried to explain.

"For each one you'd faced and beaten, there'd be another to
take his place," Ole Devil pointed out, ignoring the other's
words. "Only it wouldn't have stopped just between you and
those six. The men of Company C like and respect you enough
to want to take your part. Once that happened, the rest of the
New Orleans Wildcats would have felt obligated to stand by
their own. Mister, the Republic of Texas's Army has more than
enough problems without stupid, pointless feuds among its
ranks." He raised his right hand as his subordinate made as if
to speak. "I know, I took an ungentlemanly liberty by interfering in your private affairs. But, *Lieutenant* Dimmock, we're not
gentlemen anymore. We're *officers,* responsible for the lives of
the men under our command. And, as *you* asked to come into
my company, you're under *my* command. That gives *me* the

right to interfere and take whatever steps I feel are necessary if something's happening that could put you and the rest of my company in jeopardy." Pausing for a few seconds to let his meaning sink in, he finished, "If *I'd* had the slightest doubts about your courage, I wouldn't have taken you into Company C—or be asking if you'll volunteer for a dangerous assignment?"

"I will, sir," Dimmock agreed, looking slightly abashed as he conceded that his superior had made very good sense.

"You'd better hear what it is, first," Ole Devil warned. "It will mean going into the middle of the Mexican Army—"

"I'll still go," Dimmock declared. "And thanks—for everything."

"Come on," Ole Devil said, satisfied that he had achieved his purpose. "I'll tell what else we're going to do as we go back to the tents."

"Whooee!" the lieutenant exclaimed, when he had heard what they intended to do. "That will be something, if we can pull it off."

Before Ole Devil could make any reply, they heard bugles blowing the alarm from the other regiments' camps.

"The Mexicans are coming!" yelled a voice, and the cry was taken up elsewhere.

"Do you know something, Mr. Dimmock," Ole Devil drawled, displaying no alarm. "I had a feeling this was going to happen."

8
A THREAT TO
EL PRESIDENTE'S LIFE

"This is our third day out and still no sign of the Mexicans," remarked Lieutenant Paul Dimmock as he rode with Ole Devil Hardin and Tommy Okasi in a westward direction just before noon on the sixth of April. Then a wry grin came to his face, and he went on, "There doesn't even seem to be hide nor hair of that bunch who caused all the fuss around San Felipe the night before we left."

"Very wise and ancient Nipponese saying—" the Oriental began.

"Which he's just made up," chorused the two Texians.

"—It is better to be assailed by a thousand imaginary attackers than one who is real," Tommy finished, refusing to be put off by the interruption.

"Is *that* a *wise* saying?" Dimmock inquired of Ole Devil, although they both knew to what the man was referring.

Every section of the Republic of Texas's Army assembled around San Felipe had stood to arms all through the night in question, but no attack was made. In fact, apart from voices calling insulting messages and threatening the wrath that would descend very shortly, there had been no evidence of hostile presences in the vicinity. Only a few of the Texians had been perceptive enough to notice that the callers' broken English accents were more like those of Anglos impersonating Chicanos than Mexicans employing a foreign tongue. Some of the more discerning had put this down to a deception on the part of white renegades, several of whom were known to be serving *Presidente* Antonio Lopez de Santa Anna, who had no desire to let their countrymen know they were there.

A few others knew, or suspected, the truth.

Being both shrewd and determined, Corrinne Hallistead had not merely been content to hope that there would be no further incidents between the Texians and the New Orleans Wildcats. Instead, working with a willing "Deaf" Smith, she had concocted a plot based upon her questions regarding how the news that Mexicans were in the vicinity would be received. The two scouts who had helped Ole Devil disperse the crowd after the duel were told to ride out of the town and return to raise a false alarm. Then, to make sure that everybody remained at their posts, the aged chief of scouts and his men had been responsible for the various challenges and threats from the darkness. Finally they had come back shortly after dawn claiming that they had been searching for the enemy, who had now withdrawn and were too far away to make pursuit worthwhile.

Such was Smith's reputation that nobody thought to question his report. Even those who had suspected what really happened, Ole Devil being one of them, realized that he had acted for the best and that no harm was done. In fact so successful was the ruse that the contretemps of the previous day had been forgotten, or at least ignored.

Having been taken into Corrinne's confidence, without divulging the truth, Colonel Jules Dumoulin had convinced his regiment that there was no prospect of battle ensuing and that they would probably have a greater chance of seeing action when they arrived at Harrisburg. So they had been too busy making the final preparations for departure to find further opportunities to create friction with their Texian compatriots.[1]

1. One person who had cause to be grateful for the success of Corrinne Hallistead's scheme was *Maître d'armes* de Lepage. When he was informed

In accordance with his orders, Ole Devil had left early in the morning following the disturbed night. Once clear of San Felipe and satisfied that they were not being observed, he, Tommy, and Dimmock had separated from Company C. They had not gone far in their usual attire.

Although Ole Devil had bowed to Mangrove Hallistead's superior wisdom on the matter and had in fact never seriously contemplated that they should try to penetrate to the center of Santa Anna's force disguised as Mexicans, he had known there would be little hope of achieving their purpose dressed in the uniform of the Texas Light Cavalry. Having been involved in much fighting since the previous year's successes, his regiment was well known to their foes. In his and Dimmock's case, avoiding recognition had simply entailed changing into other, readily available garments.

Unfortunately Tommy Okasi's features were certain to arouse curiosity no matter how he dressed. In consultation with Hallistead, he had produced a most satisfactory solution. With the aid of the entertainer and certain items obtained from the local pharmacist, he had concocted a very effective brown stain.[2] Ole Devil had been amazed by the change that was made by its application, by wearing a wig of long and lank black hair, and by donning the appropriate clothing.

As Hallistead had observed, although lacking a "hawk" nose, Tommy's facial characteristics were closer to those of an Indian than a Mexican. The effect of the curious trait known as the shovel incisor—whereby the inner surfaces of the upper

of Ole Devil Hardin's warning, he had known he was expected to ignore it. However, realizing that he would not have any of the advantages an adherence to the *code duello* might otherwise have offered, he used the "threat" of a Mexican attack as an excuse to avoid visiting the Texian and issuing a challenge.—J.T.E.

2. At the beginning of the War of Secession, 1861–65, Tommy Okasi gave the formula for the concoction to the Confederate States' secret service. Belle Boyd, the rebel spy—some details of whose career are recorded in various of the author's "Civil War" and "Floating Outfit" series—found it to be of the greatest assistance during her assignment, which is told in *The Blood Border.*—J.T.E.

teeth were concave, as though scooped out—combined with the folds of the fleshy lids that gave his eyes their slanted aspect, made him look, after his skin had been tinted to a dark coppery bronze, passable as a member of the former ethnic group. The impression was increased by the wig, held back by a red headband, a multihued shirt, buckskin trousers, and moccasins with knee-high leggings.

While it might have been argued that the Oriental's *daisho* was unlike any known form of Indian armament, Ole Devil hoped to avoid close enough contact for questions to be asked about them. Tommy's bow—which he was carrying unstrung through two loops attached to the left side skirt of his big brown gelding's low-horned, double-girthed saddle—was almost double the length of the type used by red archers, but there was nothing noticeably different about the quiver of arrows hanging across his back so that the flights would be accessible to his right hand. Only the unique Japanese patterns of points on the shafts might have given a warning, but they were out of sight.

For their part, Ole Devil and Dimmock wore high-crowned black Mexican sombreros with large and curly brims, buckskin shirts and trousers, the legs of the latter hanging outside their Hessian boots. Like Tommy, they had retained their own saddles and weapons. In that day and age, neither the arms on their belts nor the second pistol and saber suspended from the saddlehorns were so unusual as to arouse comment. An innovation that was fitted to each rig, although it had not yet come into general use in Texas, was a leather "boot" to carry a rifle—its butt pointing to the rear for easy withdrawal on dismounting—strapped to the near side skirt. This effectively concealed the more unusual aspects of Ole Devil's Browning Slide Repeating rifle.[3] Only one thing might have been seen that was out of the ordinary. On the rear of his waist belt was a leather pouch containing three loaded magazines for the latter weapon.

Traveling westward, the three young men had followed a

3. New readers can find a detailed description of the Browning Slide Repeating rifle in Appendix A—J.T.E.

route parallel to and just out of sight of that which had been taken during the withdrawal. They had kept a careful watch on the surrounding terrain but had seen no sign of human life. The area they were traversing had been deserted by Texians and Chicanos. Nor did even the advance guard of the Mexican Army appear to have reached it. Guided by Dimmock, whose home was a few miles to the northwest, the trio had crossed the Colorado River the previous night and were continuing with their as yet abortive quest. At that moment they were out in the open and making for the shelter offered by some woodland.

Glancing at the lieutenant, Ole Devil felt relieved by the change in his spirits. Despite the fact that he had accepted that the way in which the Creoles had been dealt with was to the benefit of everybody concerned, he had grown moody and uncommunicative. It was obvious that he still felt deeply disturbed by the thought that he had left some good friends behind when escaping from the massacre at Goliad and was worried about how other people might regard his actions. For the first two days he had been so preoccupied that Ole Devil had wondered if including him in the party had been such a sound idea after all. However, his comments suggested that he might be coming out of his depression.

"I've another saying, just as ancient and wise," Tommy said in an almost matter-of-fact tone, but stiffening slightly and swinging his gaze to a large grove of post oak trees something over a quarter of a mile to the south. "If a man speaks of evil, it comes to him."

"At least it's no *worse* than most of *your* ancient and wise sayings," Ole Devil declared, with no greater show of emotion, as he looked in the direction indicated by his smaller companion.

"What do we do, run?" asked Dimmock, duplicating the actions of the other two. "With a head start like this, they'll never catch us."

Studying the grove that had drawn their attention, Ole Devil silently conceded that the remark had merit and justification.

Several riders were emerging from the grove, going eastward. All appeared to be well mounted and sat their horses with easy capability. Armed with pistols, knives, and lances, they had on the *charro* clothing of vaqueros. However, there was nothing to indicate whether they were friendly Chicanos or members of the Mexican Army. Vaqueros had left their haciendas to serve in the forces of both sides, and many who supported the Texians carried lances. Furthermore there was a third alternative. They could be *bandidos,* taking advantage of the present disturbed state of affairs to gather loot and plunder.

Only one thing was obvious. The score or so horsemen had not become aware of the trio's presence before riding from the grove. Catching sight of Ole Devil and his companions, they seemed indecisive as to what line of action to pursue. In the forefront of the party was a tall, slender man on a magnificent palomino gelding. If the elegance of his clothing and the quatity of silver inlaid on his saddlery was any guide, he was not only the youngest but the most wealthy of them. Pointing at the three Texians, he turned and spoke excitedly to the stocky, older rider at his right side and received either a refusal or an objection to his proposal.

"We'll talk," Ole Devil decided, bringing his big black gelding to a halt. Keeping hold of the split-ended reins in his left hand, he elevated it and its mate to shoulder level. "If they'll let us, that is."

There was nothing rash or unconsidered about the young captain's decision. As always he had studied the situation and planned in the light of his deductions. From what he had seen and deduced, he felt justified in taking the calculated risk.

Based on his observations of the riders' appearances and behavior, every instinct Ole Devil possessed suggested that they were members of Santa Anna's force. Their attire was not that of the Mexican Army's regular cavalry, but many volunteer regiments had been recruited to help put down the rebellion. The behavior of the two men in the lead implied that they could belong to such a regiment. Frequently when the owner of a hacienda allowed his son to take vaqueros for enlistment, he included an older employee to act as adviser and controller of the rest.

There were indications that the party were neither Chicanos

raiding west of the Colorado River without having reported
their intentions to Major General Samuel Houston nor a gang
of marauding *bandidos*. In either case they would have been
carrying at least some of their belongings with them. Apart
from serapes, there was nothing strapped to the cantles of their
saddles and the three packhorses that accompanied them were
equally devoid of burdens. It would be a poor bunch of
bandidos who had come so far without acquiring any loot, or a
remarkably trusting group to have left their property in the
care of the other members of their band.

Having such a good lead, the trio could almost certainly
outrun the newcomers. However, Ole Devil saw there were
disadvantages in making an escape. In warfare, as in nature, to
flee was a sign of weakness that invited pursuit. If, as he believed, the party were Mexican soldiers, there might be more of
the enemy in the vicinity. He and his companions could find
themselves trapped between two or more groups. Assuming
they were allowed to surrender, they would find it difficult to
explain why they had felt it was necessary to flee from their
"allies," which they could pretend to be as they had the renegade's passport. Even if they evaded capture, the district would
be aroused and their task made that much more difficult.

So, having taken all these points into consideration, Ole
Devil was hoping to avoid a long chase, which—even if unsuc-
cessful from the pursuers' point of view—would tire the horses
and warn the enemy that Texians were in the neighborhood. He
believed that, given an opportunity, he could lull the Mexicans'
suspicions and provide a satisfactory explanation of his party's
presence.

When Ole Devil had visited General Houston's headquarters
to collect the document upon which the success of his assignment depended, he had discovered that there was an amend-
ment to the scheme. Since he had been given his instructions,
the general had contrived to have several notices printed on the
government's official stationery. By displaying one of them and
the passport he had taken from the dead renegade, the young
Texian felt sure that he could avert any difficulties caused by
the unfortunate meeting.

After the brief conversation the youngest and wealthiest of
the Mexicans yielded to the orders, or advice, of the leathery-
faced man by his side. Instead of increasing their pace so as to
attack the trio, they continued to ride forward slowly. All but
the youngster scanned the surrounding terrain warily. He had
eyes only for the Texians and the disguised Oriental, and his
right hand rested on the hilt of the high-quality rapier that was
hanging at his left side.

"Stay here and be ready to run," Ole Devil ordered sotto
voce, setting his mount into motion.

"I hope he knows what he's doing!" Dimmock said with a
breath, watching the captain riding toward the Mexicans.

"Devil-san *always* knows what he's doing," Tommy declared
reassuringly.

"*Saludos, señores,*" Ole Devil greeted, signaling for the black
to stop about thirty feet from the leading riders. He had been
ready to turn and depart hurriedly at the first hostile gesture,
but none was made. They, too, reined in their mounts and he
continued in Spanish, "I have news of the greatest importance
to deliver to His Excellency *Presidente* Antonio Lopez de Santa
Anna. Can you direct me to him, please?"

While speaking, the Texian was watching the youngest of the
riders rather than the older, tough, and capable-looking vaquero at his side. No rebellious Chicano of his age, class, and
inexperienced appearance could have avoided showing resentment and hatred at the mention of *el Presidente*'s abhorrent
name. No such emotions came. There was only puzzlement
over hearing such a pronouncement being uttered by an obvious *Americano del Norte.*

"And what would a gringo want with the *presidente* of Mexico?" demanded the youngster, his accent that of a well-bred
Creole.[4]

"As I said," Ole Devil replied, feeling confident that his as-
sessment of the party's status was correct. "I have news of the
greatest importance and urgency to deliver to him."

"And who might you be?" the youngster challenged.

4. *Creole:* in this connotation, a Mexican of pure Spanish blood.—J.T.E.

"My name is Sidbourne Halford," Ole Devil introduced, lowering his right hand slowly to take the renegade's passport from his shirt's breast pocket and riding forward with it extended. "This will prove what I say."

"So you're a *renegade?*" the youngster sniffed, his attitude one of antipathy. He examined and returned the document.

"I *work* for *el Presidente,* much to his satisfaction," Ole Devil replied, his voice taking on a note of indignation, as he replaced the passport in the pocket. "Whom have I the *honor* of addressing?"

"Lieutenant Carlos Catañeda y Abamillo, of the Third Company, the Zacatecas Lancers," the youngster replied, impressed by the *Americano*'s air of haughty self-assurance. It was well known that *el Presidente* employed a number of gringo renegades, and some were said to be high in his favor. Such a man could make life unpleasant for a junior officer who offended or delayed him. "And what might this *important* news be?"

"Something that His Excellency would not wish to be known by too many people," Ole Devil declared, detecting a timbre of uncertainty and worry under the apparently arrogant delivery of the question. Then, conveying the impression that he was magnanimous enough to grant a favor, he went on, "If you and your sergeant will come a short way with me, I can show you why I must reach His Excellency quickly."

"Very well," Abamillo consented after glancing at and receiving a nod of confirmation from the hard-eyed vaquero.

Although the second man had not spoken, he had kept an unwinking gaze fixed on Ole Devil's face throughout the conversation. The Texian doubted whether he was sufficiently well known to members of the Mexican Army to have been identified. Not only did the sombrero cover the hornlike tufts of hair, but he had not shaved since leaving San Felipe and was far from the trim, smart figure normally seen by the enemy. However, he was aware that the vaquero would be the one he must convince. To try and exclude the man from the disclosure would arouse his hostility, so he had been included in the invitation.

Accompanying the two Mexicans a few yards from the rest

of their party, Ole Devil extracted the top sheet from the bundle of notices that were in his saddlepouch along with the original document. Passing it to Abamillo, he sat back on his saddle and, although apparently completely at ease, waited expectantly.

"Madre de dios!" the youngster exclaimed, reading the message printed in his native tongue. "Look at this, Hernandez!"

"As I said, señor," Ole Devil remarked calmly, as the vaquero was taking the sheet "It *is* important news, and His Excellency would *not* want something like that made public."

"Huh!" Abamillo sniffed, but he looked decidedly uneasy and his voice lacked conviction as he continued, "Nobody would pay any attention to such a thing!"

"Well, of course, *you* would know the feelings of the army far better than *I* do," Ole Devil answered, the words expressing more than a hint of sarcasm. "In *my* opinion the Texians' offer is a threat to *el Presidente*'s life. Somebody who has lost a kinsman or friend at the Alamo might consider getting paid so much money to kill him an attractive way of taking revenge."

"The gringo's right, Don Carlos," the vaquero declared. He had concealed his feelings better than the youngster when he had read that the government of the Republic of Texas would pay the sum of ten thousand pesos to "any member of the Mexican Army who executes the bloodthirsty tyrant and oppressor of the people, *Presidente* Antonio Lopez de Santa Anna." "There *are* some who might be willing to try to collect such a large bounty."

"Where would the foreign land thieves get hold of so much money?" Abamillo asked, being unwilling to admit before an *Americano del Norte* renegade, even one who apparently was loyal to *el Presidente,* that any Mexican would contemplate such base treachery.

"They already have it," Ole Devil replied, confident that he had guessed correctly about which of the pair was the more dangerous. The vaquero's contribution to the discussion might not have been great, but its outcome depended upon him rather than the youngster. "And as they know the money will be worthless to them whether they win their independence or are driven out of Texas, they consider it is being put to good use in the form of a reward.''

"How do *you* know so much about their sentiments?" Abamillo demanded with the air of one who had sprung a trap.

"It's my *duty* to find out such things," Ole Devil countered, his attitude implying impatience and a belief that the conversation should be brought to an end so he could be on his way. "Now, señor, if you'll be so good as to tell me where I can find His Excellency, I'll get to him as quickly as possible."

"So you work for *el Presidente,*" the youngster scoffed. "But you don't know where to find him."

"Not exactly," Ole Devil agreed, throwing a look of resignation and warning at Hernandez. "I've been with the Texians' army since just before the start of the siege at the Alamo. So I'm not certain of exactly where His Excellency might be at the moment. I'll find him, all right, but I thought *you* could shorten the time it will take me."

"We'll do better than just tell you," the vaquero promised, coming to the decision that Ole Devil had hoped for. "We'd better have six of our men take them to His Excellency, Don Carlos."

"We'll be grateful for a guide," Ole Devil declared, realizing that Hernandez was taking a sensible precaution no matter how unwelcome it might be to him. "But there's no need for you to send so many men."

"It will make us feel better to know that you get there safely," Hernandez stated. "So they're going with you—unless you've any objections."

9

I COULD HAVE RUINED
EVERYTHING

"It's a pity that those damned foreign land thieves daren't stop running away for long enough to give us a chance to get at them," the thickset, surly-featured vaquero announced loudly to the other four enlisted men of the Zacatecas Lancers, throwing a provocative glance to where Corporal Moreno was standing talking with Ole Devil Hardin, Lieutenant Paul Dimmock, and Tommy Okasi. "Then we'd soon make an end of them. But courage like *that* isn't to be expected from gringos."

Although the last thing Ole Devil had wanted was to be given an escort to make sure that he and his companions arrived at the main body of *Presidente* Antonio Lopez de Santa Anna's army, there had been no way he could avoid it. Sergeant Hernandez had been adamant, and Lieutenant Carlos Catañeda y Abamillo had accepted his guidance in the matter. As it had clearly been a choice between accompanying the six vaqueros or being taken prisoner and, in all probability, shot on the spot, the Texian had yielded to the first alternative.

Satisfied that he had taken precautions against possible trickery or treachery, Hernandez had asked for information about the country through which Ole Devil's party had passed. Having a shrewd idea of the Mexicans' purpose in the vicinity, the

Texian had claimed there was a ranch house about ten miles to
the northeast and, while its owners had fled with most of their
belongings, there were a number of horses and a fair-sized herd
of cattle grazing nearby. It was, he had continued to Abamillo's
obvious interest, a well-kept property that would be most suitable for a young man wishing to start a hacienda after the
"foreign land thieves" had been driven out of Texas. From the
lieutenant's comments, he intended to investigate the situation.

Having ensured that the majority of their captors would be
kept out of the way, Ole Devil had also been successful in
preventing a reduction in the size of his party. When Abamillo
demanded that Tommy act as guide, Ole Devil had refused. He
had pointed out that Santa Anna might want to make use of the
little "Northern Creek Indian's" services and would want to
know why they were not available. Knowing that many senior
officers were looking out for desirable properties, Hernandez
had not wanted that to happen and advised his superior accordingly.

Once the journey had been resumed, Ole Devil had turned
his thoughts to ridding himself of the unwanted escort. He had
dismissed the idea of merely trying to escape. Even if they had
succeeded, it would have had the same undesirable effect as if
they had escaped at the first meeting. Furthermore, having lost
their charges, the vaqueros would rejoin their companions.
Hernandez was no fool and would realize they had been
tricked. So he would waste no time in delivering a warning to *el
Presidente*.

With escape ruled out, the Texian decided to employ trickery. He believed two items were in his favor.

Firstly none of the escort knew the supposed reason why the
trio had been sent to Santa Anna. While Hernandez had returned the reward poster to Ole Devil, he had neither shown
nor mentioned it to any of his men. So, as far as they were
aware, they were doing no more than delivering a trio of renegades to report to *el Presidente*.

Secondly the Texian had noticed the sullen reluctance of the
men selected by the sergeant. So he had deduced that none of
them were pleased to have been given such an assignment. That

had become increasingly apparent the farther they had gone from their superiors. While the five enlisted men had not resorted to actual abuse as they were riding along, it had been made very clear that they were turning their resentment toward Ole Devil and his companions. However, while the burly Corporal Moreno obviously shared the other vaqueros' sentiments, he was a loud-mouthed braggart who enjoyed the sound of his own voice. So Ole Devil had had no difficulty in persuading him to talk and had learned much that was of interest. The more he had heard, the greater had grown his confidence that they would be able to achieve a separation in a way that would prevent repercussions.

One important item had been that, for some unexplained reason, Santa Anna's force was traveling some five miles south of the withdrawing Texians' line of march and had started to cross the Colorado River that morning. There was another piece of news that Ole Devil felt would be helpful to his plans for losing the escort. In spite of the colonists' refusal to carry out Major General Samuel Houston's "scorched earth" policy, the large army of Mexicans were having great difficulty finding sufficient food to sustain them. With the exception of *el Presidente* and his staff, the whole column was on short rations. It was that point, even more than a natural truculence and an inborn antipathy toward any kind of foreigner, that was causing the escort's bitterness.

Listening to Moreno's boasting, Ole Devil had confirmed his suspicions about the status of the Zacatecas Lancers. They were a volunteer regiment only recently recruited from vaqueros employed on the haciendas of that state. Eager for action, they had arrived too late to participate in the siege at the Alamo Mission. Like the New Orleans Wildcats at San Felipe, they had soon become bored with inactivity and disillusioned by the passive role they were playing. Furthermore, they were not used to being as short of food as they had found themselves during the march to the east. Needing to quieten the growing disenchantment among his men and prevent wholesale desertion, their colonel had taken to sending out platoons on combined scouting, foraging, and, if the opportunity presented itself, looting missions.

Now that their turn had finally come, with the prospect of at least two days away from the dreary routine of the uneventful pursuit, none of the six vaqueros relished the prospect of a premature return to the main body. A keen judge of human nature, Ole Devil was confident that he could persuade them there was no need to do so. Nothing he had seen of them led him to assume that they were sufficiently disciplined to stick rigidly to orders of which they disapproved. So he had decided to make his attempt when they reached the woodland that fringed the Colorado River and were resting their horses prior to crossing its cold and uninviting waters.

Using the skill that in later years would make him a capable diplomat, Ole Devil prepared his ground carefully. After expressing his loyalty to Santa Anna and his disdain for the fleeing Texians, he hinted at a means by which the escort could rejoin the rest of their platoon instead of making the chilly swim and long ride to the main body. While suggesting that Moreno told Hernandez that they had turned over the gringos to a patrol they had met, he noticed the other five Mexicans talking quietly and furtively together. Then the surly-looking vaquero, who had been the most vociferous in complaining about the assignment, made his provocative remark. There was no doubt that he had intended it should be heard by Ole Devil, Tommy, and Dimmock.

"You're right about that, Orlando," agreed a thickset, scarfaced man, also eyeing the trio in a challenging fashion as he and his companions walked forward. "I've never met a gringo, or an Indian, who could fight worth a damn."

Studying the approaching vaqueros, Ole Devil could tell that they were up to no good. Only two of them were carrying lances, but the remainder were fingering either the pistols thrust into or the knives sheathed on their belts.

One thing was obvious to the young captain: If the quintet were bent on mischief, and their behavior suggested that was *very* likely, Moreno was not the man to stop them. In fact the way he stepped aside indicated that he had guessed their intentions and was prepared to give them his full support.

"Look at that bunch down at Goliad," sneered one of the pair who had retained his lance instead of leaving it stuck in the ground. Tall, lean, and dandified, he was the youngest of the vaqueros and was obviously determined to convince the others of his toughness. Swaggering ahead of his companions, with the weapon held in the "high port" position in front of him, he went on, "There were over four hundred of them and they gave up without firing a shot. Then on Palm Sunday, from what I heard, they went to their knees crying like women and begging Urrea's men not to kill them. All except the ones who ran away and left the rest to—"

By sheer misfortune, from Ole Devil's point of view, the speaker was directing the mocking words at the one member of his party who was most susceptible to such taunts.

"You damned liar!" Dimmock roared, springing forward.

Having spent the past eleven years in Texas and with Chicanos for companions, the lieutenant spoke their language even more fluently than his superior. Ole Devil had learned it from a Spanish sailor during a two-year voyage on his father's merchant ship. So Dimmock had been equally able to understand all that was being said. What was more, he had realized that his superior was trying to relieve them of the escort's undesirable attendance. With that in mind, galling as it might be, he was prepared to allow the two older vaqueros' comments to pass unchallenged. However, the dandy's reference to the incidents at Goliad had proved more than he could swallow.

The lieutenant knew that a number of the men belonging to the ill-fated Fort Defiance contingent, himself included, had been willing to make a fight of it when the Tamaulipa Brigade had first come upon them. They were overruled by Colonel James Walker Fannin, who had claimed that General José Urrea would be more inclined to show them mercy if no casualties were inflicted upon his force.

What was more, when the column of prisoners had been waylaid, they were being taken to what they were led to believe was freedom. As Dimmock had seen, those who survived the

devastating volley of rifle fire from the woodland on either side
of the trail had defended themselves as best they could. They
had gone down fighting with bare hands against the bayonets of
their infantry ambushers and the sabers of the cavalrymen who
were supposed to be escorting and protecting them. The
twenty-seven men who had escaped the slaughter had done so
by battling their way clear at considerable risk to themselves.

The massacre had had a traumatic effect upon Dimmock.
Nor had it been lessened by the unfounded hints from the
young Creoles in San Felipe. Being selected to take part in such
a potentially important and very dangerous mission, by a man
for whom he had the greatest admiration, had done much to
reassert his self-respect. He had known that neither Ole Devil
nor Tommy Okasi harbored the slightest doubts about his courage. Nor did they condemn him for having saved his life instead
of dying with his comrades-in-arms.

Over the past two days the lieutenant had almost lost the
nagging sense of guilt that had been with him ever since his
flight from the ambush. The dandy's words had brought it
flooding back again. Nor, in spite of realizing they had merely
been uttered as a means of taunting a gringo, rather than an
actual participant of the massacre, could he prevent himself
from responding.

Moreno might not be the most intelligent of men, but he had
been sufficiently knowing to deduce his subordinates' intentions
and realize that there could be unpleasant consequences to be
faced later. So he had moved clear, meaning to let them deal
with the unwanted trio. Then, if there should be repercussions
because of the killing, he would be able to lay the blame on the
five vaqueros.

Listening to Dimmock's comment, the corporal began to understand what it implied. No renegade would have shown such
fury and called young Antonio a liar over the remark.

Which suggested the three men were not what they claimed!

They must be spies for the foreign land thieves!

By the time Moreno had reached his conclusion, all hell was
breaking loose.

For all his desire to impress his older and more mature com-

panions, the young dandy, Antonio, was so startled by the malevolent expression that had accompanied Dimmock's furious
denial that he came to an immediate halt. Before his mind
could fully comprehend the implications of what had been said,
the enraged Texian was upon him. Two hands clamped hold of
the lance, wrenching it from his unresisting grasp. An instant
later, its wooden shaft was smashed with considerable force
into his face. Pain erupted through him, numbing his senses.
Toppling backward, he sat down spitting blood and a couple of
shattered teeth from his mouth.

Sharing Moreno's concern for what might happen when the
matter was reported, the rest of the enlisted men had allowed
Antonio to precede them. They hoped that he would succeed in
goading the trio into some hostile gesture and so supply them
with an excuse to take action. However, like him, none of them
had anticipated such a rapid and violent result. So they were
taken unawares and found that their troubles were only just
beginning.

Instead of being caught unprepared, the would-be victims
were reacting in a way that showed they had anticipated the
need to do so.

Even without being able to speak much Spanish, Tommy
Okasi's experience in dangerous situations had allowed him to
draw the correct conclusions from the five vaqueros' threatening behavior. He had already realized that his party could not
hope to carry out their assignment as long as they had an escort
of Mexicans. So he had been waiting to discover how his employer meant to deal with the problem. As a precaution, acting
in a casual manner, he had raised his left hand to apparently
scratch at his right shoulder near the knot that connected the
supporting straps of his quiver.

When Dimmock launched the attack upon the young dandy,
the Oriental had no further need to wait for instructions. He
knew exactly what must be done and how to do it. Gripping the
projecting tip of one strap, he tugged at it, and the knot disintegrated fluidly.

"Banzai!" Tommy roared, and, as the now liberated quiver

fell from his shoulders, darted to meet the four advancing vaqueros.

As they were walking forward in Antonio's wake, being much more knowledgeable on such matters, the quartet had formed a line and moved until a short distance separated one from another.

At the right of the rank the second man to retain his lance began to turn its head forward. Next to him Orlando—the surly-faced instigator of the treacherous plot—was bringing a knife from its sheath with a speed that suggested considerable proficiency in its use. Nor was the scar-faced vaquero who was third in the line much slower and less adept in producing a similar weapon. Either because he lacked his companions' ability or because he preferred to do his fighting at more than arm's length from his foes, the Mexican on the left started to tug the heavy-caliber flintlock pistol from his belt.

In spite of the fact that he carried a firearm on his person, Corporal Moreno elected to fight with his knife. He knew that he could bring it into action with greater speed than the cumbersome handgun allowed. So he swept the spear-pointed[1] blade free and made Ole Devil his objective. Although he discovered that the Texian was turning and starting to arm himself, the burly noncom was not unduly perturbed on seeing which weapon was being chosen. He felt confident that his knife was much faster than any pistol.

Undeterred by the fact that the numerical odds were against him, Tommy once more displayed how effectively he could perform *laijitsu* and wield the *tachi* when it was drawn. There was one major difference from his demonstration to the two New Orleans Wildcats in the hollow at San Felipe: Now the Oriental was in deadly earnest! Tommy was thinking and responding like that most deadly of fighting men, a Japanese samurai.

During the brief period in which he was advancing to striking distance, the small warrior watched the quartet registering their amazement at the speed with which his *tachi* was leaping

1. Spear point: one where the double edges of the blade come together in symmetrical convex arcs.—J.T.E.

from its bamboo sheath. He did not intend to allow them to recover from their consternation.

Acting almost too swiftly for the eye to follow, Tommy brought the *tachi* around as he was coming to a halt in front of the two central vaqueros. Apart from their lethal purpose, his movements had almost the symmetrical elegance of a classical ballet dancer. For all that, in passing, the razor-sharp blade disemboweled Orlando. Then, before the intestines that had gushed from the stricken man's wound had reached the ground, the weapon reached the scar-faced man. It laid open his throat and came close to taking off his head.

To give the Mexican on the right credit, he recovered from his shock with commendable speed. While he was too slow to prevent his companions from being killed, he was determined to avenge them. Giving a snarl of rage, he lunged and thrust his lance in the Oriental's direction. Somewhat slower, the last of the quartet managed to liberate his pistol and began to draw back its hammer.

Accepting that there was no longer any hope of tricking the Mexicans into allowing his party to continue the journey unescorted, Ole Devil was just as ready for action as Tommy and equally capable of defending himself. Nor did he hesitate about the choice of weapon with which to do it. They were going to cross the river a good three miles north of the point at which Santa Anna's force had gone over. According to Moreno, there were no other patrols in the vicinity. So he could use the pistol without the shot attracting unwanted attention. Provided, of course, that he could bring it into operation quickly enough.

For all his original rage, Dimmock did not allow it to blind him to the rest of what was going on. Remembering that his victim was only one of six enemies, he knew that the affair was far from ended. Seeing Tommy rushing to meet the four vaqueros, he realized where his help was most needed. Nor did the way in which the Oriental dealt with Orlando and the man with the scar cause him to revise his opinion. Going by Antonio without a second glance, the lieutenant tried to decide which of the remaining pair required his attention most urgently. From the look of them, each was posing a threat to Tommy's life.

While the corporal was drawing the knife, Ole Devil's right hand turned palm outward and closed around the butt of the Manton pistol. Being aware that the handgun was primarily a close-quarters defensive weapon that could be kept readily available, he had devoted considerable thought to how he might best exploit such qualities. Employing a sequence of motions similar to those by which gunfighters in later years would perform the "high cavalry twist" draw,[2] he extracted the barrel from its broad retaining strap on his belt.

Moving forward with the knife held ready for a gut-ripping slash, Moreno saw the muzzle of the Texian's pistol twisting in his direction in a way he had never envisaged as possible. The unconventional method of handling the weapon did not end there. Instead of operating the hammer in the accepted fashion, the heel of Ole Devil's left hand flashed across to meet and push it to the fully cocked position. Nor did he raise the pistol to eye level and sight at arm's length along the barrel, but thrust it ahead of him only slightly higher than his waist.

Even as a realization of his peril was assailing the corporal, Ole Devil's right forefinger squeezed the pistol's trigger. So excellent was the manufacturer's craftsmanship that the hammer fell without disturbing his instinctive alignment. The shot crashed out and, above its smoke, he saw Moreno's head snapping back under the impact of a .54-caliber ball between the eyes. While the Mexican's legs continued to advance, the knife flew from his grasp, and his shoulders tilted rearward.

Without knowing it, Tommy was solving Dimmock's dilemma. While he was striking down the two men, he did not forget their companions. A rapid glance in each direction warned him from whence he faced the greater and more urgent danger. Seeing the man on his left driving the lance at him, he flipped himself sideways and down. Nor did he move any too soon. The weapon's diamond-section head almost touched his neck as it passed above him.

Deftly breaking the fall with his left hand, Tommy was al-

2. For a detailed description of how the "high cavalry twist" draw was performed, read *Slip Gun.*—J.T.E.

ready turning the *tachi* upon his assailant. Such a sinuous, almost whiplike motion was made possible by the pliancy of the magnificently-tempered steel from which it had been manufactured.[3] While he was doing so, having assessed the situation, he allowed the hilt to rotate until the blade was parallel to the ground. Instead of attempting to cut, he sent it out in an equally effective lunge.

Passing between the Mexican's ribs, the point of the blade— what European cutlers might refer to as a "reverse-Wharncliffe"[4]—pierced his heart. His momentum, combined with the strength and sharpness of the steel, caused it to pass onward until the circular *tsuba* hand guard met his chest. Knowing he could not retrieve the *tachi* in a hurry, Tommy released it. Dropping the lance and dying as he blundered onward, the vaquero collapsed across Orlando's crumpled body.

Showing none of Ole Devil's speed and dexterity, the remaining Mexican nevertheless had now drawn his pistol. However, he was fumbling in his attempt to cock it. The fact that he had seen three of his companions killed by the little "Indian" while one of the Texians had shot Moreno and the other was rushing at him carrying Antonio's lance was not conducive to steady nerves. He tried desperately to swing the weapon in Dimmock's direction, but caught a movement from the corner of his eye. Looking around, he discovered there was a further menace threatening him.

Temporarily deprived of the *tachi,* Tommy was anything but defenseless. Rolling onto his back, he flipped himself erect and whipped the shorter, but only slightly less effective, *wakizashi* from its sheath. There was, however, no need for him to use it.

Allowing himself to become distracted ruined any slight

3. See footnote 4, Appendix B.—J.T.E.
4. Reverse-Wharncliffe point: Where the cutting edge joins the back of the blade in an upward convex arc. The normal "Wharncliffe", also called a "beak" point—said to have been developed by the Earl of Wharncliffe during the sixteenth century, although variations of it have been produced since at least ancient Roman times—is now mainly used on pocketknives and has the generally unsharpened back of the blade making a convex arc to the cutting edge.—J.T.E.

chance the last of the quartet might have had to take one of his
assailants with him. Handling the lance almost like a pitchfork,
Dimmock plunged it home. There was a brief shock of agony
for the Mexican as the point pierced his chest and went
through to burst out at the rear. Stumbling backward, he
dragged the shaft from its wielder's hands and sprawled lifeless
to the ground.

Hurt though he was, anger put motion into Antonio's limbs.
Starting to rise, he saw Ole Devil swiveling to face him and
snatched out his knife. There was no hesitation in the way the
Texian responded, nor was he inclined to harbor thoughts of
mercy under the circumstances. Not only had the youngster
been a willing participant in the plot to murder his party, the
very nature of his assignment precluded the taking of a prisoner.

Dropping the empty pistol, Ole Devil sent his right hand
across to the concave ivory hilt of the James Black bowie knife.
As the weapon emerged, he hurled himself at the youngster. A
muffled scream burst from Antonio as the massive blade swept
his own knife aside and became buried into his heart.

Drawing the knife free as his victim fell backward once
more, Ole Devil looked to make sure his companions had come
to no harm and did not need his assistance. Tommy was obviously uninjured and stood retrieving the *tachi* from the vaquero's torso. Although Dimmock also appeared to have come
through the fracas unscathed, there was a worried expression
on his face as he walked forward.

"I'm sorry, Captain Hardin," the lieutenant said. "I could
have ruined everything, letting myself be goaded like that."

"We'd have had to fight them anyway," Ole Devil replied
consolingly. "They meant to kill us, and the way you acted
gave us an edge."

"Perhaps—" Dimmock began, still showing more perturbation than relief at learning his superior did not blame him for
his actions.

"Forget it, Paul," Ole Devil ordered. "Now that they're
dead, we can go ahead with letting Santa Anna find out what's
in store for him."

10

THEY HAVE TO BE
CONVINCED IT'S GENUINE

"So that's what the great *el Presidente* looks like!" Lieutenant Paul Dimmock said with quiet vehemence as he lay between Ole Devil Hardin and Tommy Okasi peering cautiously over the top of a ridge. "Well, I've always heard that he was a fancy-dressing son of a bitch, and it's true."

Having disposed of the six vaqueros' bodies, weapons, and such of their belongings as had not been required by sinking them in a deep backwater on the Colorado River, the Texians and the Oriental had made preparations to continue the assignment. Selecting the three best of the dead men's horses so that they could conserve the energies of their own mounts, they had unsaddled and liberated the rest. On their home range the animals would have returned to the hacienda, causing concern over the whereabouts of their absent riders. Being in a strange area, particularly when going home would entail swimming across a river, they were unlikely to go in search of the Zacatecas Lancers' remuda. So, at least until their companions returned from the abortive search for the ranch, the escort would not be missed.

With the majority of the traces of the fighting obliterated, Ole Devil had led his party eastward. Although the afternoon was well advanced before contact was made, locating their quarry had presented no great difficulty. Dimmock's local knowledge had supplied a clue when he remembered there was a reasonable trail to the south. All that had been necessary was for them to take precautions against another unwanted meeting. On two occasions they had seen small bands of Mexicans in time to avoid detection. Wearing sombreros and serapes that had belonged to their victims as a minor disguise in case they should be noticed from a distance, they had finally attained a position from which they could carry out an unobtrusive surveillance.

"That's him, all right," Ole Devil agreed in no louder tones, conceding that his subordinate's second remark was justified. "And he's still up to his old trick of leading the parade."

"He's not taking as much care as the last time we saw him," Tommy remarked, referring to a reconnaisance mission carried out by Ole Devil, Lieutenant Mannen Blaze, and himself earlier in the year. "Nor are the soldiers around him. We'd never have got so close that earlier time."

"That we wouldn't," Ole Devil confirmed, studying the trail something under half a mile away.

Riding well in the lead of his command, *Presidente* Antonio Lopez de Santa Anna was surrounded by his thirty-strong bodyguard of Popocatepetl Dragoons, resplendent in their shining helmets and breastplates. They were followed by his ornate carriage and the two big wagons carrying the luxuries with which he invariably kept himself supplied.

On his own behalf, as became one who was pleased to regard himself as "the Napoleon of the West," *el Presidente* cut a fine figure mounted on his high-stepping thoroughbred white stallion, its saddle and bridle glistening with embellishments of precious metals. Middle-aged, clean-shaven, and not unhandsome, he had a well-knit figure that was improved by artificial aids. His attire that day was based upon the uniform of the marshal of France circa 1804. The black bicorn hat had more than a sufficiency of heavy gold-lace edging, was decorated by a plume of ostrich feathers imported at considerable expense, and bore a massive golden Mexican-eagle insignia. Heavily embroidered with gold wire in the shape of oak leaves, his dark-blue coatee also sported enormous epaulettes of the same material. White breeches, now stained by the day's travel, were tucked into black Hessian boots. A gold cloth sash and a well-polished black weapon belt supporting a sword reputedly worth seven thousand U.S. dollars completed his far from modest ensemble.

As Tommy had said, if the leisurely and casual way in which they were moving was any guide, Santa Anna and his retinue felt confident that there were none of the enemy within miles.

"The rest of the column don't seem to be taking any better precautions," Dimmock commented, turning his gaze from the glittering array of military ostentation. "And they aren't anywhere near as fancy-looking either.

Although *el Presidente* and his bodyguard might convey the impression that they were leading a triumphant parade, the mass of men who were following some distance behind clearly did not share their sentiments. The ragged, plodding lines of foot, horse, and artillery were paying just as little attention to their surroundings. However, they appeared to be too dispirited to care what might befall them. Bringing up the rear came the baggage train of pack mules and creaking, lumbering oxen-drawn carts. It seemed woefully small in comparison with the number of soldiers who were dependent upon its contents.

"If you'd been through what they have," Ole Devil drawled, also studying the main column, "you wouldn't be feeling any too happy with life either. They had it rough all along and it's getting rougher by the day."

"You sound almost sorry for them," Dimmock stated.

"I am, for the enlisted men," Ole Devil admitted. "Most of them didn't want to join the army."

Despite all the fervor with which el Presidente and his generals had assembled the force to march north, and notwithstanding its recent successes, the corruption and basic instability of his regime was taking effect. Already impoverished by years of civil war, interfactional feuding, and officials lining their pockets, the Mexican treasury was unable to produce the finances for the venture. The money was procured by enforced "dona-

tions," or through loans at usurious rates of interest,[1] but much
of it was squandered on nonessentials, and little went to purchase badly needed supplies or equipment.[2]

As early as during the siege at the Alamo Mission, the various shortages had been the cause of much suffering and numerous desertions among the recently conscripted men. Now even
the better-quality regiments of regular soldiers were feeling the
pinch. Their previous actions had been fought in the warmer
lands farther south. So they were ill prepared to cope with the
far from clement weather of a Texas spring.

To the various *Activos* battalions, inexperienced and barely
trained "reservists" forcibly enlisted for the duration of the
campaign, the conditions were barely tolerable. What small im-
provement had accrued to their spirits during the "victory"
celebrations after the fall of the Alamo Mission was being
wiped out by the hardships of the march. Being foot soldiers,[3]
they were unable to forage with the facility of the cavalry. En-
grossed in that necessary adjunct to survival, the latter were
paying little attention to what should have been their duty of
providing a screen against Texian reconnaisance or raiding parties.

Comparing the column with one that he had studied just

1. Messrs. Rubio and Errazu, moneylenders, supplied four hundred thou-
sand dollars at an interest rate equivalent to *forty-eight* percent per annum.
They also obtained as security the entire proceeds of a forced loan on four
Mexican departments, *plus* all duties from various customs houses and the
right to import certain military supplies duty free. With their connivance,
General Manuel Fernandez Castrillón secretly "donated" a large portion of
his personal fortune at the more "generous" four percent interest a *month*.
—J.T.E.

2. For example, General Antonio Gaona cornered the market on various
essential supplies along the line of march and sold them at a one hundred
percent profit. Colonel Ricardo Dromundo, one of *Presidente* Santa Anna's
brothers-in-law and appointed master purveyor for the column, never even
offered to account for the large sums of missing money with which he had
been entrusted to purchase provisions.—J.T.E.

3. The Arizona Hopi *Activos* Regiment, which appeared in the early books
of the "Ole Devil Hardin" series, were in fact, a privately recruited volunteer cavalry unit and not "reservists" in the accepted sense.—J.T.E.

north of Monclova during the first week of February, Ole Devil could see that it was greatly reduced in numbers. Even then it had not struck him as being in the best of condition. His report to that effect had been one of the factors upon which Major General Samuel Houston had based the decision to let the stand at the Alamo Mission take place. Clearly there had been great losses through casualties and, in all probability, desertion. However, those who remained still greatly outnumbered the Republic of Texas's Army.

From his examination Ole Devil felt confident that, provided his party could accomplish their assignment, the odds could be reduced. Nor would he allow his sympathy for *el Presidente*'s underfed and badly clothed conscripted civilians prevent him from trying to carry out the task.

"It's a pity we didn't bring our rifles," Dimmock remarked, returning his attention to Santa Anna's retinue.

"Why?" Ole Devil asked.

"We could fire a couple of shots at him and run for it," the lieutenant explained.

"The bullets would barely reach the trail at this range," Ole Devil pointed out. "And firing would let them know there are enemies nearby."

"It would bring the escort after us, all right," the lieutenant conceded. "But we ought to be able to make it back to the horses before they catch us."

"Ought to isn't good enough," Ole Devil said grimly. "When we make our move, it has to be a lot more certain than that. Our instructions from the 'government' look authentic, but they'll have to be convinced it's genuine before they'll do as General Houston wants. Letting them get it too easily won't do that."

"Would the honorable gentlemen care to hear an ancient and wise Nipponese saying unworthy self has just made up?" Tommy inquired, twisting around to scan the terrain behind them. He continued without waiting for an answer. "Person who spends too much time watching others may be seen himself."

"I hate to admit it, but 'unworthy self' is right," Dimmock

informed his superior with mock resignation. "As long as we were on the move and didn't let them come too close, anybody who saw us would probably take us for foragers. But they'd know we weren't if they saw us lying here."

"I'd never have thought of it myself, though," Ole Devil answered, pleased to see that the lieutenant did not resent the rejection of his suggestion and wondering if his recovery from the gloom cast by the taunting from the youngest vaquero had been caused by the excitement of being at such close proximity to the Texians' supreme enemy, or through the prospect of action in the near future. "There's nothing more for us to see, and we can't do anything here. We'll go and take a look at what's ahead."

"Unless I've got it wrong, the trail goes through some woodland about three or so miles ahead," Dimmock announced, as the trio withdrew carefully from the ridge. "But even if they reached it before sundown, they'd be too late to go through in daylight and wouldn't want to after dark. So I'll bet on them making camp by the creek that's just this side."

"Let's find out if your memory's as good as it was about the trail," Ole Devil suggested with a grin that showed he felt sure that it would be. When satisfied that they could not be seen by the Mexicans in the column, he straightened up and went on. "We might find what we need on the way there."

The trio's horses had been left in the concealment offered by a small draw about a quarter of a mile from the ridge. As they were approaching, they heard the animals start to give snorts of alarm.

"Something's frightening them!" Dimmock barked, bounding forward as his companions also increased their pace.

Swiftly as the Texians advanced, the Oriental outdistanced them. By the time they reached the top of the draw, he was already dashing down the fairly steep slope with the sure-footed agility of a bighorn sheep. However, their attention was directed at the bottom.

Although none of the horses had managed to tear free the reins by which they had been tethered to bushes, it was plainly only a matter of seconds before at least some of them would.

All were rearing, or backing away, in attempts to divest themselves of the restraints placed upon their movements. Nor was the cause of their behavior hard to locate.

"Hot damn!" Dimmock exclaimed, skidding to a halt and staring at the predatory beast that was causing the horses' alarm as it stalked them through the bushes at the other side. He grabbed at his pistol's butt. "Look what it is!"

"Don't fire unless we have to!" Ole Devil warned, duplicating the lieutenant's action in spite of realizing their predicament.

Being so close to the trail, as Ole Devil was all too aware, there was a danger that shooting would be heard. If it was, it would be investigated. For all that, he did not ignore the possibility that the need to use the pistol might arise. They might be compelled to do so to save Tommy's as well as the horses' lives.

The carnivore with which they were contending was undoubtedly feline, but of a kind that only rarely came so far north into Texas. If it had been a mountain lion, the usual inhabitant of that region, the situation would have been much less serious. Although adequately equipped to do so, members of the species *Felis concolor* were disinclined to face opposition from human beings. Seeing the Oriental approaching, a cougar would almost certainly have turned and fled.

Unfortunately the animal was *not* a mountain lion.

With such a thickset build and the yellowish hide marked by black rosettes, it could only be a jaguar! Its very size and marking ruled out the faint hope that it was the smaller and less dangerous ocelot, which was the only other possible contender.

Heavier and far more aggressive than the cougar, a jaguar was much less likely to be frightened away from potential prey by the sight of a human being.

Nor was it!

Giving a low, coughing roar, the jaguar abandoned its stalk and hurled itself in Tommy's direction. The sight of it caused the horses to redouble their efforts to escape. One of the vaqueros' mounts broke its reins and bolted along the bottom of the draw, but the rest were unable to do so.

"Get down there and catch it!" Ole Devil snapped, grasping his Manton pistol and never taking his eyes from the Oriental.

Sharing his employer's awareness of the possible repercussions of using a firearm to save the animals, Tommy hoped to remove the need. While he had never seen such a beast as the jaguar, he knew how other members of the cat family were prone to make an attack. So he felt that he could cope with the situation, even though his method would place his life in jeopardy.

Such a minor consideration would never sway a samurai from his purpose.

Satisfied that he had diverted the jaguar away from its intended prey and upon himself, Tommy came to a halt and whipped out his *tachi*. Even without the need for conscious thought, he was following the dictates of his Bushido training. Confronted by a worthy and dangerous enemy, a samurai met the challenge with his body squarely to the front, the right foot forward and left drawn back. Although he grasped the hilt in both hands, the right above the left, he did not raise the *tachi* beyond the level at which its point would be in line with a human opponent's throat.

Having adopted his posture of readiness, the little Oriental waited until the huge animal—its one hundred and twenty pounds' weight not much less than his own—launched itself upward in a spring. It came hurtling at him, mouth open to expose the tearing fangs and legs outstretched to employ an even more effective armament.

To the watching Texians it seemed that Tommy intended to let the jaguar impale itself upon the *tachi*. He had considered and discarded the idea. While adopting it would achieve the desired result, it would not kill silently enough for his purpose.

At the last instant, when to Ole Devil and Dimmock it seemed Tommy must be caught in the grasp of the beast's great curved and needle-pointed claws, he swung his left leg in a pivoting step which carried him just—and only just—out of danger. As he was doing so, he raised and brought down the *tachi* in a similarly rapid motion. Biting into the back of the jaguar's neck as the animal's body was being carried impotently past Tommy by the momentum of the abortive spring, the blade decapitated the jaguar. Although the headless carcass landed with a thud and the limbs thrashed spasmodically, there was no other sound.

Allowing the *tachi* to fall from his grasp and replacing it with the *wakizashi,* the Oriental darted toward the still-struggling horses. He had noticed the one that had escaped and knew what must be done. So, before Dimmock could descend the slope and carry out Ole Devil's order, Tommy reached the animals. Grasping his mount's split-ended reins in his left hand, a slash from the *wakizashi*'s razor-sharp blade severed them just above the knot by which they were secured to the bush. Having done so, he discarded his second weapon and, catching hold of the saddlehorn, vaulted onto the plunging brown gelding's back. Showing superb riding skill, he turned and sent it racing after the fleeing horse.

Seeing that Tommy had that aspect under control, Dimmock ran to and started to calm down the rest of the animals. Having paused to see whether the disturbance had been heard and attracted unwanted attention, Ole Devil hurried after the lieutenant to lend him a hand. They had brought their mounts under control when the Oriental returned at the successful conclusion of his pursuit.

"He was going up the side, but I stopped him before he reached the top," Tommy announced. "While I was up there, I looked over. If anybody heard the horses, they aren't bothering to come and see what caused it."

"That's fine," Ole Devil replied. "Go and keep a look out, though. We'll stay here until the horses are fully recovered, then we'll push on."

Even as he was speaking, Ole Devil glanced at the body of the jaguar. If it had not been for the Oriental's quick grasp of the situation, his courage, and his skill with the *tachi,* their mission could have received complications that would have made it impossible to complete.

11

I'LL HAVE TO MAKE
THEM MOVE

"There's the sentry," Ole Devil Hardin said with a breath, halting and peering through the darkness. "Standing between the two wagons!"

"Here," answered Tommy Okasi, in no louder tones, holding out his longbow, which was now strung and ready for use, "I'll take care of him."

Unfastening and lowering the quiver of arrows to the ground, the Oriental slipped the *wakizashi* from its sheath. Then he went forward with the intention of removing an obstacle to the mission he and the Texian were hoping to accomplish.

Once the horses had recovered from their fright, Ole Devil, Tommy, and Lieutenant Paul Dimmock had wasted no time in setting off to conduct a further reconnaisance of the area. Still using the dead vaqueros' mounts and leading their own, they had been able to travel at a much faster pace than *Presidente* Antonio Lopez de Santa Anna and his column. Picking a route that offered the most opportunities to avoid being seen, while keeping as close as possible to the trail, they had maintained an even more careful watch upon their surroundings. They had seen no further signs of the enemy, but did not regret the extra effort the precautions had entailed.

As there had not been anywhere suitable between the draw and the woodland for what they meant to do, Ole Devil had decided to utilize the remaining short period of daylight to find out what the terrain beyond the trees might offer. He had agreed with Dimmock that Santa Anna would halt for the night on reaching the small creek, but he wanted more information before considering how to deal with the situation. The assignment upon which they were engaged was of great importance, and he did not intend that they should fail through a lack of foresight. So the trio had pushed on. After covering about three quarters of a mile, they had emerged onto rolling and fairly open range. In the distance the trail disappeared from view after ascending what the lieutenant had claimed was a very steep slope.

With the darkness closing in, although Ole Devil had questioned Dimmock about the nature of the ground on either side of the ascending section of the trail, the three young men had not attempted to make a visual inspection. Instead, they had sought for a safe haven in which to spend the night. As Ole Devil had pointed out, while the Mexicans were unlikely to march through the woodland before morning, some of them were sure to enter for the purpose of gathering fuel or in search of food. So making camp in the shelter of the trees was out of the question.

Fortune had favored the trio. Noticing a fold in the ground not too far from the edge of the woodland, they had discovered that it would satisfy all their requirements. There was good grazing for the horses and a small stream to supply water, but the surrounding terrain would make it difficult for anybody to approach undetected.

Giving thought to the prevailing conditions and to what he intended to do, Ole Devil had ordered that the horses were to be unsaddled and hobbled. While restricting their movements and preventing them from straying far, the latter would allow them to rest and graze far more adequately than if they were secured in any other way. Not until the hobbling had been completed, using strips cut from the serape Dimmock had been wearing, had he and his companions attended to their own needs.

While making a meal from some of the jerky,[1] which was the only food they had brought with them, Ole Devil had informed his companions of what they were going to try to do that night. It was an audacious, carefully considered, and anything but ill-conceived scheme. Dimmock had not been pleased to learn that he was being assigned to a passive role, but he realized it was one that could not be omitted.

It might have been possible to approach and even enter the Mexicans' encampment on horseback, but the primary purpose of the visit could only be achieved on foot. So Ole Devil had elected to make the whole of the journey in the latter fashion, which had meant that somebody must stay behind and take care of the animals. He had also pointed out that Tommy alone possessed the necessary skill as an archer to fulfill his intentions. Hoping to be allowed to accompany the Oriental, the lieutenant had hinted that, as senior member of the party, it was Ole Devil's duty to delegate such a dangerous assignment to those of his subordinates who would be less of a loss if things went wrong.

"At least," Dimmock had concluded hopefully, "that's what I've always been told is the ranking officer's responsibility."

"Rank doesn't only have its responsibilities, Paul," Ole Devil had countered in a gentle tone that robbed the words of any sting. "It has its privileges, too, and that's why I've picked me to go instead of you."

Carrying some of the "reward posters" and the original document supposedly issued by the Republic of Texas's government, although Ole Devil had hoped that neither would be

---

1. Jerky: Beef, or various other kinds of meat, cured by stripping the animal's hams in a manner that left a thin membrane covering each approximately one-inch-thick segment. The portions were dipped for a moment in a strong boiling brine solution, then smoked briefly before the curing process was completed by exposure to the sun. The result, if done correctly, was a nourishing, palatable, long-lasting, easily transportable food that was very sustaining against fatigue.—J.T.E.

required, he and Tommy had made their way toward the Mexicans' encampment. The Oriental was carrying his bow, and the quiver of arrows, which had hung from his saddlehorn while he was wearing the now discarded serape and sombrero, on his back. For his part Ole Devil retained the borrowed garments and had the Browning Slide Repeating rifle, a magazine installed, across the crook of his left arm.

As Ole Devil had anticipated, there had still been a number of foraging parties among the trees. However, none of them had shown any indication of going far enough to continue their searching in a way that might take them to the horses. One of the factors he had considered was that, provided the foragers did not hear the animals, there was nothing on the open range to make them feel it was worthy of investigation. On the other hand the noise the foragers had been making enabled them to keep out of their way. Their presence had even made the final stages of the task easier. The few sentries who were posted had seen nothing suspicious about two men coming from the woodland.

Even before they had reached the shallow creek, Ole Devil and Tommy had been able to identify their destination. The large striped marquee that Santa Anna had been using during the reconnaisance of February had been set up close to the opposite bank. What was more important, his quarters, the large tent behind them serving as a kitchen, his personal carriage and baggage wagons were separated from the rest of the encampment by his bodyguard of Popocatapetl Dragoons' remuda and bivouac.

Nor had arriving in the immediate vicinity of *el Presidente*'s headquarters posed any great problems for the intruders. By choosing an area of darkness between the glows of two fires, they had waded unnoticed across the creek and had circled around to approach by what they considered to be the most advantageous route. Having anticipated the presence of sentries, they had kept a careful watch and discovered that one was posted between them and their objective.

There were, Ole Devil and Tommy realized as they studied the sentry, certain factors in their favor. In the first place the sentry was neglecting his duty. Positioned between the wagons to keep watch for intruders like themselves, he was standing and looking in the opposite direction. His gross dereliction was made worse by the fact that he had leaned his carbine against the side of one vehicle so he could bury his hands in the pockets of the cloak he had on. Secondly, disposing of him was made easier because of the way he was dressed. The Dragoons only wore the heavy metal helmets and breastplates when mounted or if *el Presidente* wished to impress some important guest he was entertaining. So the man had only a cloak, tunic, and thin shirt to protect him.

Advancing with great stealth, Tommy drew his conclusions as to how the removal of the sentry could be achieved. One thing was obvious. Whatever the means employed, it must be done with the minimum of noise.

Only seventy-five yards beyond the inner end of the baggage wagons, completely unaware that two enemies were so near, Santa Anna was entertaining members of his staff to dinner. They were in the well-illuminated marquee, gathered around a table laden with food. Although he did not consider his guests sufficiently important to rate the sentries wearing full-dress uniforms, the table was covered by a white-lace cloth and set with his fine monogrammed china crockery, silver tea or coffee pots, sparkling wineglasses, and crystal decanters.

Nor, despite the fact that the rest of his force was so poorly provided for, did *el Presidente* seem worried by the possibility of it being seen that he had a far superior standard of provisions; unless he was relying upon the errant sentry to keep off any spectators. The flaps at the center of the side wall nearest to the wagons were drawn back to form a door through which the servants could come and go.

Nearer and ever nearer crept Tommy, blessing the fact that his disguise had called for him to wear moccasins. They allowed him to move even more silently than would have been possible with his Hessian boots. Oblivious of his peril, the sentry continued to gaze enviously at the glow of light and listen to the sounds of cheerful conversation. He was to pay a very high price for his behavior.

Having come close enough, the Oriental struck with deadly efficiency.

Clasping his left hand over the sentry's mouth, Tommy succeeded in drawing back the head as well as preventing any outcry. Working with smooth coordination, the right fist passed the *wakizashi* over the man's shoulder. The turned-up collar of the cloak might have been capable of keeping the wind from the back of his neck, but it offered no protection against the attack. Swiftly Tommy's blade sank into the area at the base of the throat and just above the collarbones that gave access to the windpipe. A quick slash, a spurting of blood, and in a few seconds it was all over. Nor, apart from a soft scuffling as the stricken sentry struggled briefly and futilely, had there been anything to be heard.

Lowering the lifeless body of the Dragoon to the ground, the Oriental moved forward a few steps. There was nothing to suggest that the killing had been seen or heard. However, as he gazed through the open flaps of the marquee, he gave a low hiss of annoyance. Although Santa Anna was seated facing the opening, he was practically concealed by two of the men on the nearer side of the table. Dealing with him as had originally been arranged was no longer possible, but Tommy felt confident that the difficulty was far from insurmountable.

Although neither the Oriental nor Ole Devil had ever heard the word *psychology,* they possessed a practical working knowledge of its application. Before leaving on the mission, Tommy had made a selection from the various kinds of Japanese arrows that were with his other property in the Texas Light Cavalry's baggage train. An expert *kyudoka,*[2] he had considered that one fitted with a *wata-kusi* point would produce the most satisfactory effect.

Studying the situation, Tommy realized that he could not employ a *wata-kusi* with *el Presidente* seated in such a manner. However, he had yet another kind of shaft, which he believed could solve the dilemma.

2. *Kyudoka:* A practitioner of *kyudo,* archery in the Japanese fashion.— J.T.E.

While the Oriental was carrying out his reconnaissance, Ole Devil rolled his victim's body beneath the left side wagon. Then the Texian took up a position that he hoped would make anybody who happened to look into the dark space assume he was the sentry.

Rejoining his employer, Tommy picked up but did not immediately swing the quiver across his shoulders. Instead, while whispering a description of what he had seen in the marquee, he took an arrow from the right side and laid it carefully on the ground.

"I'll have to make them move," the Oriental concluded, extracting the extreme left shaft from the quiver. "And this ought to do it."

"It ought," Ole Devil agreed, having identified the arrow's type from the shape of its head and knowing its purpose. "Is there anything I can do for you?"

"Only one thing," Tommy replied, donning the quiver. "Make sure that no dishonorable person comes up behind unworthy self before I've finished."

Taking up the bow with his left hand, the Oriental made it ready for the task he was about to begin. Holding the *wata-kusi* in his right palm so that the shaft pointed down at a rearward angle, he fixed the nock of the second arrow to the string. Then he returned along the gap until he was as near the end as possible without allowing himself to be seen from the marquee or by anybody on either side of the wagons.

Drawing the bow with a technique far different from that employed by Occidental archers,[3] Tommy halted the rearward motion when the hollow point of the forty-inch-long arrow was almost touching the extended forefinger of his left hand. In the very formalized Zen style of *kyudo,* hitting the target was considered secondary to the correct movements of the arms, bow, arrow, and cloak. So taking sight and loosing could require anything from five to twenty minutes. However, the Oriental

3. The technique employed by Tommy Okasi is described in *Young Ole Devil,* and a comparison with two Occidental methods can be made by reading *Bunduki.*—J.T.E.

was a practical warrior and did not indulge in the placid art-istry of Zen. The aim he took, while careful, was swift.

By releasing his hold on the string and the nock of the shaft, Tommy allowed the bow's powerful flexed limbs to propel the missile forward. Almost immediately the special function of the *hiki-ya* point made itself known in no uncertain fashion. In addition to being hollow, the head had holes drilled along its sides like those of a flute. Once it was in flight, the air passing through them acted in the same way as blowing into the mouthpiece of the musical instrument.

One advantage gained by having the handle set two thirds of the way down the stave, as opposed to centrally in the fashion of other countries, was that such a position made it possible for men of comparatively short stature to wield such lengthy and puissant bows. Another was that it allowed an arrow to be dispatched with very flat trajectory over considerable dis-tances.[4]

However, on this occasion, Tommy directed his shaft upward at a gentle angle and did not make use of the latter quality.

Hearing the rising crescendo of the whistling caused by the air being forced through the *hiki-ya*'s holes, the men at the table looked around. Before they could discover what was mak-ing the eerie noise, the arrow pased over their heads almost too quickly for the human eye to follow. Slitting the canvas, it disappeared out of the marquee's roof, and the sound died away as its pace decelerated until it fell to the ground.

Although used primarily for signaling, the *hiki-ya*'s banshee-like wailing whistle could also be employed in the hope of pro-ducing a disturbing psychological effect upon the enemy.

---

4. Some of the archery competitions at Kyoto's Sanju-San-Gen Do temple took place in special covered galleries one hundred and thirty-two yards in length and only twenty-two *feet* high. The idea was to discharge as many arrows as possible and have them reach the other end without hitting the cross beams. It is recorded that in 1696, during a session lasting for twenty-four hours, a samurai called Wasa Daichera shot eight thousand one hun-dred and thirty-three arrows—at a rate of five to seven a minute—of which *three thousand two hundred and thirteen* flew the full length.—J.T.E.

Tommy's arrow achieved the secondary function to his entire satisfaction!

Chairs went flying and crockery or glasses were discarded, regardless of their value, as the occupants of the marquee rose hurriedly and in alarm.

None of the party were sure of what had happened, but all sensed that it presaged some kind of danger. Every man's concern was to find a safe place, rather than trying to discover who —or what—was threatening him. So each adopted his own method of trying to evade whatever further peril might be forthcoming. The erstwhile relaxed and jovial group disintegrated into individual bodies flinging themselves away from the no longer attractive open flaps in the wall.

Displaying the kind of rapid thought and action that had helped bring him to his position of power and authority, Santa Anna wasted neither a second nor a motion when the guests who had been between himself and the unseen menace sprang in opposite directions and left him exposed. Without worrying about the damage he would inflict upon his highly prized property, he overturned the table and flung himself flat on the ground behind it. While the wood was thin and would offer only minimal protection, he was at least hidden from the mysterious assailant's view.

El Presidente had not taken his evasive action any too soon!

Allowing the second arrow to slip forward through his grasp as soon as the first one was in flight, Tommy nocked it to the string. He was trained to shoot almost as rapidly as the legendary Wasa Daichera (see footnote 4), and although he was under the stress of being in combat, the conditions were not so exacting as when the great samurai *kyudoka* had performed the famous feat at the Sanju-San-Gen Do temple in the city of Kyoto.

In spite of hearing startled shouts rising from the tents occupied by Santa Anna's bodyguard, and the sounds of sentries raising the alarm from their posts on the other three sides of the marquee, Tommy refused to be flustered. He drew and, changing his point of aim to attain a flat trajectory, loosed the shaft. This time there was only a savage hiss, which seemed almost muted when compared with the ear-piercing screech of the *hiki-ya.* Flying almost parallel to the ground, the arrow struck just above the center of the table that was sheltering *el Presidente.* It punched through the wood and flew on, but its momentum was so reduced that it was stopped as the three hawk feathers of the fletching struck the canvas of the wall at the back of the marquee.

Pandemonium reigned both outside and within Santa Anna's quarters, but none of his guests offered to leave and investigate. The protection offered by the striped walls of the tent might be inadequate, but at least it served to keep those inside concealed from the archer in the darkness.

As he saw the first of the sentries run around the end of the marquee, Tommy reached for another arrow. Pure chance rather than deliberate intent made him select another *wata-kusi.* Clearly a man of quick thought and discernment, the Dragoon started to make for the wagons instead of going to the open flaps to ask for instructions from his superiors.

Once more, without needing to look down, Tommy went through the process of fitting the nock to the string and supporting the shaft of the arrow against the bow's handle by resting it on the base of his left thumb. By the time he had completed his draw and aim, the sentry was close enough to be able to see him. Skidding to a halt and giving a startled exclamation, the soldier started to raise his carbine.

Forward darted the Oriental's arrow. It took the Dragoon in the right breast before he could raise his weapon high enough for use. A scream of agony burst from him as he twirled helplessly around. The arrow had impaled him so thoroughly that only the fletching protruded from the front of his torso and the *wata-kusi* point extended far behind his back. The carbine slipped from his hands, and they clutched spasmodically at the feathered remnant of the missile, which was all he could reach. Sprawling to the ground, he lay shrieking and writhing in torment for a few seconds before becoming limp and motionless.

Turning as he was nocking yet a fourth arrow, this time tipped by a *yanagi-ha* point, Tommy ran back to where Ole Devil was waiting. Unlike the guard whom he had replaced, the Texian was watching his front and holding the Browning in a position of readiness. As his companion approached, he turned his head for the first time and allowed himself a brief, inquiring glance.

"It worked," the Oriental said, but did not offer any further explanation.

Nor did Ole Devil waste time by requesting one. Instead he set off with Tommy in the direction of the creek. They went so swiftly and silently that nobody noticed them taking their departure. Behind them all was confusion.

From various points in the encampment, regimental buglers were blowing the call to arms, and drummers were helping to sound the alarm.

Men bellowed questions that nobody troubled to answer and shouted orders that were ignored.

On the picket lines, particularly those of the Popocatapetl Dragoons—who were closest to the disturbance—the startled horses were demanding attention.

Neither of the remaining Dragoons on sentry duty nor such of the kitchen staff who arrived to investigate showed the grasp of the situation and the initiative of the man whose diligence had been rewarded by impalement with an arrow. Instead of attempting to seek out the intruders, they did nothing more constructive than congregate at the entrance to the marquee and goggle at the occupants, waiting to be told what to do. No instructions would be given until it was far too late for them to be of any use.

So it was no wonder that Ole Devil and Tommy made good their escape without encountering the slightest difficulty or the need to use their weapons again that night.

But had the mission achieved its purpose?

12

GET WHOEVER TRIED TO
KILL ME

Apparently, despite the forethought and skill with which Tommy Okasi had caused *Presidente* Antonio Lopez de Santa Anna to be exposed before his bow and arrow, the plan had failed.

Raising his head after several seconds had passed without any further missiles bursting through his inadequate shelter, *el Presidente* found himself looking at the hole about an inch in diameter that had not been in the center of the table when he had overturned it. A shudder ran through him as he realized how close he had been to death. The thought put motion into his limbs.

Attaining a kneeling posture, Santa Anna peered with great caution around the edge of the table. He did not care for the sights that met his eyes. Passing over the broken china and shattered wineglasses on the ground, his cold stare took in the retainers and sentries who were talking and gesticulating at the entrance to the marquee. Then he glared from side to side, noticing the inactivity of his guests. Without leaving his place of concealment, he began to give vent to the wrath aroused by the discovery that nothing was being done to avenge his narrow escape from death.

"Get outside, all of you!" *el Presidente* thundered, but he did not offer to rise and set an example. "Move lively, damn you, or I'll make you wish you had. Go and get whoever tried to kill me!"

All the assembled staff officers exchanged alarmed glances. Their military duties were so exalted of late that it was only rarely any of them were called upon to face physical danger. In fact, with a few exceptions, they had even avoided taking more than a long-range supervisory participation throughout the siege at the Alamo Mission. So not one of the party was eager to go forth and brave the dangers of the night.

For several seconds the guests' fear of the unknown menace outside—induced in part by the psychological effect of the *hiki-ya* point's eerie passage through the marquee—warred against their knowledge of how virulent their superior's wrath could be when something happened to arouse his ire.

The latter won!

El Presidente's subordinates decided, without consultation between them, that it would be more politic to take their chances by obeying him than to face the consequences of a refusal. They also realized that even if the mysterious assailant had not been frightened away now the alarm had been raised, he would be confused by the multiplicity of targets that a mass exodus would present. So, with one exception, they made for the open flaps. On passing through, each tried to keep as much of his own person as possible concealed behind some other member of the group.

Laudable as such motives might be, they were unnecessary. The intruders against whom the precautions were being taken were already some distance away and had no intention of returning.

"Are you all right, Your Excellency?" asked the guest who had not joined in the departure, hurrying toward the table with an air of solicitude. "You weren't hit, were you, *patrón?*"

Plump to the point of obesity, bespectacled and perspiring freely, the speaker for all his military raiment, did not have the look of a hardened fighting soldier. Nor did his grimy hands and slovenly appearance give any clue to his exact status as a member of *el Presidente*'s staff. However, his bearing as he approached his irate superior was that of a man who was solely concerned with carrying out his primary duty and so had no time to waste on less important tasks. Although he was also motivated by a reluctance to go outside where danger might still be lurking, he was in fact performing his main function by inquiring after Santa Anna's state of health.

Since the march to crush the rebellion of the "foreign land thieves" had been halted in January for two weeks, due to *el Presidente*—who reserved the right to make all decisions, major or minor[1]—being bedridden with dysentry, he had come to appreciate the importance, where his own welfare was concerned at any rate, of skilled medical attendance. So he had appointed Dr. Nabarro Reyes, who had finally cured his illness, as his personal physician.

"I'm all right," Santa Anna said gruffly, standing up. "What happened?"

"Somebody shot this at you," Reyes explained, having looked around to find some further excuse for remaining in the marquee. Scuttling across to the rear wall, he pulled Tommy Okasi's missile from it. Paying no attention to the way in which the point had slit a far wider gash than might have been expected from the size of the hole in the top of the table, he returned to his employer. "It's an arrow!"

"I can see that, damn you!" *el Presidente* spat out, his temper far from improved as he surveyed the damage done to the embellishments that had been on the table. Reaching to take the proffered weapon, he glanced at it, started to look away, then stared with greater intensity. *"Madre de Dios!"*

There was, Santa Anna considered, good cause for the startled exclamation and the even more profane comments with

1. Santa Anna did all his own staff work and had a penchant for issuing extremely meticulous orders. For example, when producing the plan of campaign for the final assault on the Alamo Mission, he had gone into such details as instructing the infantry regiments involved not only to have their bayonets fixed, but also that the straps of their headgear must be "under the chin".—J.T.E.

which he was about to follow it up. While he could not claim to have any extensive knowledge of archery, he was able to appreciate the implication of what he was seeing, and he did not care for it. Clearly whoever had tried to kill him was a person of diabolical ingenuity.

"Doctor!" yelled the voice of Ramón Caro, *el Presidente*'s ferret-faced and much disliked little private secretary, before the profanity could begin. "One of the sentries has an arrow through him."

"Get out here quick, man!" came the harder tones of the dandified commanding officer of the Popocatapetl Dragoons' bodyguard, Colonel Juan Almonte.[2] "He's still alive and needs you."

"Come on!" Santa Anna ordered, relying too much upon the loyalty of his bodyguard to let it appear that he had delayed the doctor from attending to one of their number who was wounded. Striding toward the entrance, still carrying the arrow, he went on thunderously, "Hurry up, blast you. I want his life saved."

Which was true enough, although not altogether from purely humanitarian motives. *El Presidente* was *very* interested in finding out the identity of his would-be assassin, and the injured sentry might be able to provide the requisite information.

Even in the faint glow of light from the marquee, which extended as far as the stricken sentry, Reyes needed only a single glance to tell him that he would be exceedingly fortunate if he could do as his superior ordered. Despite his medical capability being somewhat limited, considering the high position he was holding, the doctor had been involved in Indian attacks on two occasions. So he knew enough about dealing

2. There was nothing out of the ordinary in a full colonel having command of a mere thirty men. While it is an exaggeration to say that in the Mexican Army of the period there was an officer and a sergeant to every two men, a disproportionate number of senior ranks were available. Particularly in Santa Anna's main invasion force, a lack of commands commensurate with their rank had generals leading single battalions and colonels having to be content with the charge of even smaller units.—J.T.E.

with wounds inflicted by arrows and he doubted whether there
was any hope for the soldier.

The arrival of the Dragoons' guard commander carrying a
lantern produced extra illumination by which Reyes was able to
confirm his summation. Studying the head of the shaft that had
impaled the sentry, the doctor's far from active mind noticed
that it was not a kind he had previously seen. For all that, he
was sufficiently intelligent to deduce its diabolical purpose. He
could now also understand why Santa Anna had displayed
such agitation and consternation on being handed the identical
arrow he had taken from the wall of the marquee.

Although Reyes would never learn the true facts, he was
examining an exceptionally lethal variety of a Japanese *kyudoka*'s arsenal.[3] The *wata-kusi* point fully justified its name,
"tear flesh," being equipped with barbs of a remarkably effective kind. They were movable, lying close to the shaft during
the discharge and flight. This allowed them to produce a wide
gape, but cut down wind resistance to a minimum. Once inside
the victim's body, they opened when there was any attempt
made to draw out the arrow. It was impossible to remove them
in such a manner without increasing the severity of the injury.

"Get on with it, damn you!" Santa Anna growled, conscious
of the growing circle of onlookers and wanting to impress at
least some of them by his concern for the stricken sentry. "Do
something to help the poor man."

"I—I'll have to cut the head off and pull the shaft out the
way it went in, Your Excellency," the doctor announced, with
the anxious deference of one who was anticipating his failure to
carry out the wishes of a ruthless dictator. "But I'm afraid
doing it won't save him. In fact I doubt whether he'll even
recover consciousness for long enough to receive the last rites,
no matter what I do."

"All right, Doctor," Santa Anna answered in a milder tone,
although he had plans other than those of allowing a priest to

3. Another type of *kyudoka* arrowhead, but one that Tommy Okasi was not
carrying, is described in footnote 6 of Appendix B.—J.T.E.

attend the sentry if the soldier should regain consciousness. He gestured with the arrow he was holding. "Do what you can."

"Name of the Holy Mother!" General Vincente Filisola croaked in his native Italian tongue, staring from the missile in the sentry's body to the one in his superior's hand. Then he continued in Spanish, as befitted his office as *el Presidente*'s stodgy and generally[4] unimaginative second-in-command. "If that had hit you after going through the table—"

"Yes!" Santa Anna put in testily, having no desire to be reminded of unpleasant consequences that he had already envisaged.

Flying from a greater distance than the arrow that had impaled the sentry, and with the table acting as a further impediment, the viciously barbed head of the missile would almost certainly have remained inside *el Presidente*'s body instead of emerging on the other side. In which case, if—taking the size of the hole it had made in the table as a guide—Reyes had tried to draw it out, the two-inch-long, needle-sharp prongs would have extended and reduced any slender chance Santa Anna might have had of surviving the wound.

Not only Filisola had noticed the nature of the arrowheads. Those of the crowd who could not see were informed of the terrible devices by their more favorably positioned companions. There was some pushing and jostling as the less fortunate onlookers attempted to obtain a better view.

"Don't just stand there gaping and chattering, damn you!" Santa Anna bellowed, glaring around him furiously and waving his arrow-filled fist toward the wounded Dragoon. "Go and catch the man who did this."

Goaded into activity by his superior's wrathful demeanor and words, Almonte spat orders at the members of the bodyguard who had gathered. Told to start searching beyond the two wagons from between which the arrows must have been discharged, the guard commander reluctantly led several unenthusiastic men away. Having seen and deduced the purpose of the *wata-kusi* points, without being aware of such a

4. No pun intended, I assure you.—J.T.E.

device's name, none of them relished the prospect of hunting in the darkness for a person carrying a weapon with so diabolical a potential.

Equally eager to avoid incurring *el Presidente*'s opprobrium, the crowd scattered with rapidity. Ostensibly having the intention of informing the rest of the encampment of what had happened, but really wishing to put themselves in a safer locale for the time being, the dinner guests hurried away. Even Ramón Caro, who usually stayed close to his employer on the pretext that his services as secretary would be available if required, left with the rest. Taking the hint from their betters' behavior, the various minor members of Santa Anna's retinue who had gathered returned to their interrupted occupations.

Within a minute of *el Presidente* having made his displeasure and wish for action known, he had achieved his desire. Apart from himself, the only one who remained from the dinner party was Doctor Reyes, kneeling by the critically wounded soldier and doing what little was possible to succor him.

"He *is* coming around, Your Excellency," the physician announced with relief, although aware that the recovery was not the result of his own doing. "Perhaps he'll soon be able to answer your questions."

Dr. Nabarro Reyes might not have been the world's most competent medical practitioner, but he possessed a reasonable amount of discernment. So he was aware of why his patron was concerned over the possibility of the sentry's life being—if not saved—prolonged.

* * *

"From the sound of things," Lieutenant Paul Dimmock remarked, looking at his commanding officer and no longer able to restrain his impatience to learn if the mission had been successful, "you-all stirred up a regular hornet's nest back there."

"You might say that," Ole Devil Hardin replied, sitting on his opened-out bedroll with the Browning Slide Repeating rifle by his side. *"El Presidente*'s alive and well, but not in the best of spirits or temper, unless I miss my guess."

In spite of having crossed the creek in safety, the captain and Tommy Okasi had not been allowed to finish their journey

without interruption. Nor had they expected to be able to do
so. While they had been able to approach the encampment
without arousing curiosity, they had realized that—under the
prevailing conditions—the motives of anybody seen going in
the opposite direction would be suspect. Before they had covered a hundred yards, they had been compelled to seek the
shelter offered by a small clump of bushes. Their purpose in
hiding was twofold. First they had wanted to avoid inviting the
attentions of the sentries and the foragers who were returning
to investigate the disturbance. Second, and of equal importance, they had also hoped to learn the results achieved by their
risky expedition.

When the two intruders had satisfied themselves on the latter
point, and when several minutes had gone by without any more
Mexicans leaving the woodland, they had resumed their withdrawal. The passage through the trees had been without incident, and approaching the rendezvous, Ole Devil had warned
Dimmock of their pending arrival by whistling a few bars of the
popular ballad, "Will You Come to the Bower I Have Shaded
for You?"

As an added example of the young captain's forethought, the
countersign had been for the lieutenant to respond with the
thrilling, if bloodcurdling, strains of the "Degüello." This was
the traditional Spanish "March of No Quarter," warning of
throat cutting or other forms of merciless death, and it was said
to have been played continuously all through the final assault
upon the Alamo Mission to inform the defenders of their forthcoming fate. So it was one tune no Mexican would expect a
Texian to use.

Checking to make sure they were not being followed, Ole
Devil and Tommy had accompanied Dimmock to the bottom
of the fold. However, for all their awareness of the lieutenant's
interest in their activities, they had made preparations for
spending the night in what comfort was possible before offering
to satisfy his curiosity.

"How will that affect us tomorrow?" Dimmock asked, deciding that his superior's estimation of Santa Anna's state of mind
was accurate. "He's going to be madder than a bobcat dropped

on the lid of a red-hot stove and just as likely to come up spitting and clawing.

"But he won't be sure who he should start doing the spitting and clawing at," Ole Devil guessed. "We didn't leave any of the 'reward posters' or our 'letter from the government.' So he'll not know whether it's us or some of his own men who are after his hide."

"He'll make sure that his bodyguard are a lot more watchful tomorrow, though," Dimmock pointed out.

"Nobody in the camp will be getting much sleep tonight," Tommy commented, being occupied with removing the string from his bow after spreading his bedroll and laying the depleted quiver of arrows on it. "And, according to an ancient and wise Nipponese saying—"

"Which he's just now making up," the lieutenant said with a sigh, although he was too wise to discount any summations made by the Oriental, even when they were delivered in such a guise.

"—Man whose night has been disturbed is less wary than one who slept well and woke refreshed," Tommy finished, unabashed by the interruption. "Unworthy bodyguard of dishonorable war lord may be more wary tomorrow, but illustrious gentleman should be able to carry out his duty in spite of that."

"So *now* you know," Ole Devil said dryly. "Which of those heathenish devices did you use on the second sentry, Tommy?"

"A *wata-kusi,*" the Oriental replied, after checking the contents of his quiver. "There wasn't time to pick and choose, I just took the first that came to hand."

"I'm pleased you did," Ole Devil declared. "After seeing what one's capable of doing, his *amigos* won't be any too eager to face up to more like it. Let's get some sleep. We've another hard day tomorrow."

"Is there any danger of patrols being sent out to look for you?" Dimmock asked.

"It's not likely," Ole Devil guessed. "Like I said, Santa Anna doesn't know who tried to kill him, and I think he'd rather believe it's somebody in his command than that we 'foreign land thieves' would dare to try. And even if he does send out search parties, the way some of his men were shooting, they'll not be too eager to be wandering around in the darkness."

"I thought they were shooting at you," Dimmock said, having heard rifle fire from beyond the trees before his companions returned.

"They may have thought they were," Ole Devil grinned. "But we weren't where the shooting was being done. No, I don't think we'll have any trouble tonight."

"In that case," the lieutenant drawled, straightening up with an attitude of just too casual an ease. "I'll put the 'reward posters' and the 'government's letter' in my saddlebags ready for tomorrow and grab me some sleep."

Watching Dimmock walk away and having caught the undertone of tension in his voice, Ole Devil put it down to a slight apprehension over the task that he was to carry out on the following day. However, the captain was convinced that when the time came, he could be counted upon to behave in a satisfactory manner. When he had accomplished the assignment, he would never again need to worry about anybody casting aspersions on his courage.

Equally observant and even more perceptive than his employer, Tommy drew a different conclusion from Dimmock's attitude.

* * *

At about the time that the two Texians and the Oriental were settling down for the night, a council of war was commencing in Santa Anna's striped marquee. However, there was no longer any trace of the evening's earlier festivities. Although the table was now set on its legs, the lace cloth and its other fittings had been removed. Along with the gash left in the rear wall by the first *wata-kusi* arrow, only the holes in the roof and the top of the table served as reminders of what had happened.

Not that any such aids to memory were necessary!

Looking at *el Presidente*'s scowling face, none of the assembled officers believed he had forgotten, nor that he would be inclined to forgive after he had been brought so close to death.

"I'm sorry, Your Excellency," Colonel Juan Almonte said, opening the proceedings reluctantly as every eye turned in his direction. He was standing rigidly at attention and had the appearance of a man who expected a storm to break over his head at any moment. "But we haven't been able to find a trace of whoever tried to kill you."

"What was all that shooting we heard not long ago?" General Filisola inquired before his florid-faced and fuming superior could speak.

"It started when some damned fool in one of the bivouacs opened fire on us by accident," Almonte answered, and, hearing a muffled snigger, he darted a baleful glare to where Ramón Caro was sitting at the elegant little portable escritoire that always accompanied *el Presidente* on his travels. There was little love lost between them, and under the circumstances, the secretary's sneer was annoying in the extreme. "At least it had better have been by accident, or—"

"His Excellency was nearly killed just now," Caro pointed out, delighted over his hated rival's discomfiture and determined to wring every possible benefit from it. "And *that* wasn't by accident."

"I'm aware of what happened without having any inky-fingered letter scribbler tell me!" Almonte spat back. "Two of my men were killed—"

"And what kind of watch do these men of *yours* keep?" the secretary demanded, almost in a screech. He was furious at the way in which he had been described, but he lacked the courage to demand satisfaction for the insult. "The one who was knifed—"

"Has been doing a lot of little jobs for *you* just recently," Almonte interrupted, seeing a way to turn the tables on his antagonist. "Perhaps he'd have been more alert—"

"That's enough!" Santa Anna barked. Normally he encouraged the hostility that existed among the members of his staff and turned it to his advantage. With the possibility of there being a plot to assassinate him organized by somebody under his command, he wanted nothing to distract them from the main issue. "This is no time for petty bickering among ourselves."

"Did the wounded sentry recover and talk, Your Excellency?" Filisola asked as the rivals relapsed into sulky silence.

"He did," Santa Anna admitted, studying each of the faces around him carefully to see if any showed concern. There was none that he could discern, so he continued. "But all he could say was something about an Indian having killed him."

"An Indian?" Almonte repeated, for there were a number of soldiers in the column who qualified for such a description, and it had been near the camp of one such group where the firing had started.

"Considering that a bow and arrows were used," Caro sneered, "that isn't very surprising."

"*You* wouldn't know about such things," Almonte countered viciously. "But some of us who do have never seen Indian arrows looking like those that were used."

"Yes, but—" the secretary began, angered by the rumble of concurrence from the other members of the staff.

"Could it have been one of those damned Hopis who came back with the story about their regiment being wiped out by a gringo with a face like *el Diablo* who could call up a fire-spitting river monster?[5] Filisola suggested. "One of them might have blamed you for their bad medicine, Your Excellency."

"I've never seen or heard of the Hopis using arrows like that," objected the overweight and overdressed Colonel Ricardo Dromundo, speaking for the first time. The comment was mainly because of a natural instinct to contradict any suggestions made by other members of the staff rather than through any knowledge of such things. He looked at his brother-in-law and went on helpfully, "I could have their chief sent for—"

"I've already done it," Santa Anna answered ungraciously, once again sweeping the faces of the men with a scrutiny filled with suspicion. "Of one thing I can assure you *señores.* I mean to get to the bottom of this business. And when I find out who's behind the attempt to kill me, I'll make them wish they had never been born."

5. The explanation is given in *Ole Devil and the Mule Train.*—J.T.E.

13

SHOOT, DAMN YOU, *SHOOT!*

There was no sign of tension or apprehension about Lieutenant
Paul Dimmock as he knelt, hidden, at the right side fringe of an
extensive clump of tall, thickly growing bushes. Close by, also
in concealment, Tommy Okasi had just mounted the big brown
gelding and held the reins of Dimmock's equally large and
powerful bay. However, Ole Devil Hardin was missing. So were
the reserve mounts that had been provided by the dead vaqueros. The absence of the latter suggested why the leader of
the mission was not with his companions.

Barely a quarter of a mile away from the two young men's
hiding place, *Presidente* Antonio Lopez de Santa Anna was
approaching along the trail. Paul Dimmock and Tommy Okasi
were waiting to perform the duty for which they had traveled
many miles and endured considerable hardships, not to mention the various difficulties and dangers they had encountered.

As Ole Devil had predicted on his return from the visit to *el
Presidente*'s encampment, the party had spent an undisturbed
night. Still making use of the acquired horses, as their personal
mounts would need to be kept as fresh as possible, they were on
the move again soon after dawn. They had kept a watch to their

rear, but had not expected to see anything of the Mexican column before they arrived at their destination.

Conducting a closer examination of the steep incline over which he had expressed an interest the previous evening, Ole Devil had announced that it met with his full approval. There were a few clumps of bushes in the vicinity, and one of them might have been planted deliberately to meet their requirements. It was close enough to the trail for the plan to work and sufficiently far from the steep slope for the horses to have time to gather momentum before they made their ascent. Furthermore the ground on either side of the rising trail could only be traversed at speed by determined, well-mounted, and excellent horsemen.

Tommy and Dimmock possessed all three of the requisite qualities.

After making sure that neither the lieutenant nor the Oriental and their horses could be seen by anybody traveling eastward along the trail, even when the latter were mounted, Ole Devil had left them to keep their vigil. Before leading away the spare animals, he had shaken hands and wished his companions every success. Now he was out of sight beyond the rim, ready to help cover their flight with his Browning Slide Repeating rifle if necessary and hoping that the need to do so would not arise.

The plan would work far better if it was believed that only one Texian and an "Indian," or rather that particular "Indian," was involved. For that reason Tommy and Dimmock had discarded the sombreros and serapes.

Studying the situation when their objective came into view, the lieutenant was impressed at the further confirmation of how capably his superior could assess the way in which another person would probably react to a set of circumstances. Ole Devil had claimed that Santa Anna might consider it inadvisable to make any major or too obvious alterations to the formation and behavior of the advance party.

The summation proved to be correct.

Apart from having the bodyguard of Popocatapetl Dragoons gathered more closely around him, which was not noticeable to the men in the column to his rear, *el Presidente* had made no significant change to the order of march that had been adopted on the preceding day.

As Ole Devil had deduced from the facts that were available, much as Santa Anna might have wished to obtain the added protection they would offer, there were no scouts ahead or on the flanks of his retinue. He had not made use of them since taking up the pursuit of the Republic of Texas's Army after the fall of the Alamo Mission. It had been his contention, made to boost the flagging morale of his long-suffering soldiers, that such precautions were unnecessary, as the "foreign land thieves" were too terrified of his invincible warriors to do other than run away.

Such behavior was typical of *el Presidente*'s carefully calculated disregard for his personal safety. He was now being compelled to pay the price for the advantages it had accrued in the past.

In spite of the attempt upon his life, being experienced in such matters, Santa Anna was aware of the dangers that might ensue if he should change his arrangements. Not only would the suggestion that he was worried over his safety have an adverse effect upon the enlisted men, but it would strengthen the position of whoever was behind the abortive assassination. He held his position of complete authority because he had created a belief in his own courage. To exhibit what could be exploited, or even merely regarded, as weakness and caution could be fatal.

However, small though Santa Anna's only precautions might be, they were making Dimmock's task more difficult. As in Tommy's case when lurking outside the striped marquee, *el Presidente* was only fractionally visible between the leading members of the escort. The lieutenant knew that he did not have the same means as Tommy to scatter the Dragoons and make Santa Anna a more accessible target. Nor was there time for the Oriental to join him and carry out the scattering. Everything was too far advanced to start making any change in their plans.

Dimmock was cradling the thirty-six-inch-long, half-stocked

barrel of his borrowed Hawken Model 1830 caplock rifle upon the angle formed by a sturdy branch and the trunk of his shelter. Obtaining an added stability for the ten-and-a-half-pound firearm was important at that moment. He needed to align the buckhorn backsight and the three-sixteenths-of-an-inch "low" silver-bead foresight with great care.

The rifle had been loaned to the lieutenant by Ole Devil Hardin as a replacement for the weapon that had been taken from him after Colonel James Walker Fannin had ordered the Fort Defiance contingent to surrender at Goliad. Despite only having had it in his possession for a few days, he had already fired it often enough to be conversant with its individual traits and was competent in its use. For all that, he knew he was going to need a certain amount of luck as well as all his skill to carry out the first part of his assignment correctly.

Even when charged with its maximum load of two hundred and fifteen grains of black powder, the excellently constructed Hawken "Plains" rifle could only throw its two-hundred-seventeen-grains .53-caliber patched[1] lead ball with complete reliability up to, at the most, two hundred and fifty yards. While it would kill over at least double that distance, the farther away, the more remote grew the chances of placing a bullet exactly where it was required to go.

There was, Dimmock decided as he was estimating the range carefully, only one possible solution: Santa Anna must be allowed to reach a distance at which a hit of the kind called for in the plan could be made.

Doing this was going to place Tommy Okasi's life in some additional jeopardy, but it would not materially alter the rest of the scheme as far as Dimmock was concerned.

Looking down from his place of concealment beyond the

---

1. One of the problems when charging a muzzle-loading rifle was to ensure a tight enough fit to make the barrel's rifling grooves take effect. Ramming home a bullet large enough to achieve this was difficult and caused a decrease in accuracy due to the distortion of its shape. So a ball slightly smaller than the size of the bore and wrapped in a "patch" made from a small, well-greased piece of soft cloth or thin hide was used.—J.T.E.

ridge, Ole Devil frowned as he estimated the decreasing distance between his companions and Santa Anna's party. It seemed to him that Dimmock was delaying far too long. He frowned as he wondered if the lieutenant was intending to make a major alteration to his plan. He hoped not. Having accepted that the task could not be carried out without some risk to the participants, he had tried to reduce it as far as possible. By ignoring the instructions, Dimmock was increasing the danger and placing Tommy's life as well as his own in even greater danger than was necessary.

Suddenly a deep concern began to assail Ole Devil. Remembering the changeable way in which the lieutenant had been acting, he wondered if he had made the correct choice in allowing Dimmock to perform the assignment. After his preoccupied behavior the previous evening, the lieutenant had been a changed man since dawn. He had seemed cheerful and almost lighthearted, but not in a way suggestive that he was trying to cover fear of what lay ahead. If it had been, Ole Devil would have had no hesitation over how to act. As it was, to have refused to let Dimmock play the part that he had been promised would have aroused such resentment that he could never have regained his self-esteem.

Thinking back, Ole Devil realized that Dimmock's attitude and the way he had shaken hands when they parted by the bushes was indicative of a man who, having wrestled with a serious problem, had reached a decision and meant to carry it through at all costs.

The question was, what might the decision have been?

Bringing the assignment to the conclusion required by Major General Samuel Houston called for the plan to be carried out in the way Ole Devil had ordered. Dimmock's local knowledge had justified his inclusion in the party and, without his help, the fight against the six vaqueros might have had a different ending, but his mental state could have rendered him unsuitable for the vitally important duty that he had been given. A deviation of the kind he might be contemplating would ruin everything.

There was, Ole Devil conceded bitterly, nothing he could do to change things.

It was far too late for Dimmock to be replaced.

"Go on!" Ole Devil said with a breath. "Shoot, damn you, *shoot!*"

Almost as if he had heard his superior's silent but vehement command, Dimmock obeyed. Satisfied that he could not make a better alignment of the sights, he held his breath to ensure there was no movement to disrupt it and tightened his right forefinger.

Liberated, the Hawken's hammer descended and ignited the percussion cap!

There was a deep crack as the detonated powder in the cylinder expelled the bullet.

An instant later, about two hundred and fifty yards away, Santa Anna's bicorn hat was sent spinning from his head!

Having fired, Dimmock did not waste time in waiting to discover the result of his shot. Whatever its effect might have been, there would not be any opportunity to reload and try again. Furthermore he realized that there was only one hope of survival for his companion, and now, if he was to carry out the special task to which he had assigned himself, they must take flight without delay.

Following Ole Devil's instructions, Dimmock dropped the rifle as an unacceptable encumbrance. He rose and, without a backward glance, sprinted to the waiting horses. Grabbing his reins from Tommy, he vaulted onto the saddle and set his mount into motion. With the Oriental, who was carrying the longbow strung ready to be used, by his side, he galloped toward the slope. However, it was not their intention to make the easier ascent offered by the trail.

Confusion reigned for several seconds after *el Presidente*'s headdress was removed by the Texian's bullet. He and the whole bodyguard reined in their mounts. While he felt gingerly at his head, they stared around to find out if he, or anybody else, had been hurt. Then, attracted by the rumbling of hooves and the sight of the two riders dashing away, Colonel Juan Almonte bellowed orders. Followed by half of his men and leaving the remainder to form an even closer circle around Santa Anna, he gave chase.

"It's that 'Indian' from last night!" *el Presidente* screeched, drawing the required conclusion from Tommy's appearance and armament. "Get them, damn you, get them!"

Quivering with a mixture of rage and fright over the second narrow escape from death he had had in less than twenty-four hours, Santa Anna forgot to add a most important supplement to his order.

Urging their horses onward, Tommy and Dimmock made for the slope at an angle that would bring them to where Ole Devil was waiting to give covering fire should it be needed. Before beginning the far from easy climb, which would demand every bit of their attention if it was to be accomplished successfully, each of them glanced to his rear. As they expected, they found a party of Dragoons—some waving carbines and the others brandishing sabers—thundering after them.

In itself, the sight was neither surprising nor exceptionally alarming.

Pursuit had been inevitable no matter whether Dimmock's shot had taken effect or missed its mark completely. For all that, the situation was far from desperate. With so much of a lead—even though, because of the delay, it was somewhat less than Ole Devil had envisaged—being mounted on horses of at least equal quality to those of the Dragoons and clad in much lighter, less cumbersome clothing, Tommy and the lieutenant had an excellent chance of outdistancing their pursuers.

Provided, of course, that there were no mishaps!

Just as the two young men were about halfway to the top, something went wrong!

Apparently through an error of judgment while negotiating a particularly steep and awkward section of the incline, Dimmock attempted to correct his horse's movements. Doing so caused it to lose its footing momentarily. Thrown off balance, it slipped and started to slide back along the slope. Nor, although it recovered its equilibrium and managed to avoid falling over, could it gather sufficient momentum to resume the climb. Instead it was compelled to continue its involuntary downward progress.

Yells of triumph and delight rose from the Dragoons as they

saw the Texian's desperate predicament. There was an even
greater source of satisfaction in store for them.

In trying to turn his mount upward once more, it seemed
that Dimmock was unseated, and he toppled from the saddle.
Showing remarkable presence of mind, considering the circumstances, he snatched the spare pistol from its holster on the
saddlehorn as he was leaving the horse's back. Furthermore,
displaying such agility that he might have anticipated—or even
arranged—the mishap, he contrived to alight on his feet. While
he was no more able to prevent himself from going down the
slope than his mount had been, at least he was not making a
helpless and uncontrollable headlong plunge.

Catching a glimpse of what was happening from the corner
of his eye, Tommy took the chances involved in glancing
around to confirm certain suspicions. Satisfied that his judgment was correct, he neither tried to stop nor turn his horse so
as to render assistance. Only about half of Santa Anna's bodyguard were following, but that still made the odds at least seven
to one against them. Not that such a consideration would have
prevented the Oriental from going to his companion's aid if he
had felt the situation called for such a deed. However, being
aware of how the "accident" had come about, he was certain
that the lieutenant would not welcome such a gesture on his
part. So he returned his attention to the front and continued to
guide his mount toward the top of the ridge.

Bounding toward the onrushing enemy, Dimmock's right
hand tugged the pistol from its loop on his belt. As he had only
recently started to wear the weapon in such a fashion, he had
not acquired Ole Devil's ability to cock the hammer as it was
emerging. So it was fortunate, if somewhat peculiar in consideration of his experience with firearms, that he had been carrying
both the pistols with their actions at full cock.

There was a look of grim satisfaction and gratification, rather
than alarm at his position, on Dimmock's face as he came to a
halt at the foot of the slope. Knowing where the ball would do
most good, he raised the pistol from his belt and took aim at
Almonte.

"Death to the murderous butcher, Santa Anna!" the lieutenant yelled defiantly in Spanish, and he squeezed the trigger.

The pistol barked, and although the bullet missed its intended mark, it was not entirely wasted. Back snapped the head of the Dragoon who was riding just behind the colonel. With blood running from a hole between his eyes and the helmet ripped from his head as the lead burst out of his skull, he slid from his saddle.

"Shoot him!" Almonte almost screamed, seeing the Texian bringing the second pistol into alignment.

Even before the order was given, those of the Dragoons who were holding carbines were making ready to open fire. As they were *el Presidente*'s personal bodyguard, they were equipped with percussion-fired weapons instead of the antiquated flintlocks supplied to the majority of the Mexican Army. So all seven pieces went off in a ragged volley. However, discharged from the backs of fast-moving horses, they might have counted themselves fortunate that even one of them made a hit.

Struck in the right shoulder, Dimmock was spun around, and the empty pistol flew from his grasp. The pain sent him to his knees, but such was his grim determination to complete the assignment he had set himself that he managed to keep hold of his second weapon. Gritting his teeth, he made another attempt to shoot Almonte.

Although the colonel was fortunate enough to escape injury for a second time, he did not get off scot-free. Giving a scream as the bullet tore into its chest, his horse's legs buckled, and he had to throw himself clear as it started to collapse. Sweeping by him, his men bore down on the animal's killer.

Watching the Dragoons approaching with their burly sergeant in the lead and raising a saber, Dimmock gave a low hiss of satisfaction. Thrusting himself erect, he made what he knew was a pointless attempt to leap aside as the noncom launched a blow in his direction. Even as the blade was about to split open his skull, the lieutenant's last thought was that, after what he had just done, nobody would ever again be able to hint that he had lacked courage.

A moment later Paul Dimmock was dead!

"Catch his horse for me, one of you!" Almonte bellowed as
his men started to draw rein around the Texian's body. "The
rest, get after that 'Indian'!"

Although the Dragoons set off, none of their hearts were in
the task. Already the little "Indian" was approaching the top of
the slope. From the speed at which he had made the ascent, his
mount was superior to their own. What was more, there might
be others of his "tribe" waiting for him up there. If not, he was
still armed with that deadly bow and almost certainly had more
arrows of the particularly vicious variety with which he had
killed their comrade-in-arms the previous night.

Even those of the party who had not seen the missile in
question had had it described to them in gory—possibly
slightly exaggerated—detail. So there was a mutual, if unspo-
ken reluctance and disinclination to go where such murderous
devices could be loosed at them. However, being aware of their
fate if they refused, they decided to at least make a token appearance of continuing the pursuit and would see what developed once they reached the ridge. At least their superior would
not be there to drive them on.

Unaware of what was taking place behind him and not daring to look back, Tommy was able to see the crest of the ridge.
He found that Ole Devil was still there, staring down the slope
with an expression of bafflement and anger.

"Go on!" the Oriental called, remembering what action was
called for on his employer's part. "He let himself be killed to
make it work. Don't spoil it, or his death will be in vain."

14
OF COURSE IT'S GENUINE

Experiencing a shock as if he had been doused with cold water, Ole Devil Hardin's mind absorbed Tommy Okasi's words. They came as such a surprise that it was only by exercising all his strength of will that he found himself capable of carrying out the Oriental's instructions. However, he knew that he must do so. There would be a better chance of driving off their pursuers if they kept it from being known how many men were involved. Cursing himself silently and furiously for not having surmised what Lieutenant Paul Dimmock had meant to do, although he knew that few people would have anticipated such a gesture of self-sacrifice, he forced himself to continue with the plan he had made.

Turning, Ole Devil ran to his big black gelding. As his companion appeared at the crest of the ridge, he started the animal moving. A short way ahead lay another area of woodland, just as Dimmock had predicted, and that had been taken into consideration as part of their strategy. It was there that the Texian hoped they would be able to persuade any pursuers to turn back.

Reaching the shelter of the trees before the first of the Popo-

catapetl Dragoons made their appearance, the two young men
left their mounts tied with the three reserve horses that Ole
Devil had already taken there. Showing his usual forethought,
he had placed the animals where they could be seen, thus causing confusion as to the actual size of his party. Returning to the
edge of the woodland, he and the Oriental took up positions
behind the sturdy trunks of a couple of trees and awaited developments.

Watching as the Dragoons rode slowly over the top of the
ridge, talking and gesticulating from one to the other, Tommy
made a selection from his remaining arrows. Thrusting one into
the ground within easy reach of his right hand, he held another
in its palm and nocked a third ready for use. Waiting until the
men were about one hundred and fifty yards away, he drew and
loosed the first shaft.

Hearing the eerie whistling of a *hiki-ya* point in flight, which
lost little of its alarming qualities when discharged by day, the
Dragoons came to a halt. However, as the arrow plunged
downward and embedded itself in the turf a few feet ahead of
them, the sergeant applied the spurs to his horse. Waving his
saber, still smeared with Dimmock's blood, he charged forward. Although one of the enlisted men was in motion almost
as quickly, the rest hung back until they had gained a lead of
some ten yards before following.

"That sergeant's mine!" Ole Devil growled, cradling the butt
of the Browning Slide Repeating rifle to his shoulder and
squinting along the forty-and-five-sixteenths-of-an-inch length
of its octagonal barrel.

Knowing that no answer was expected, Tommy did not make
one. Nor was he surprised at his employer's choice. Having
seen the sergeant cut down Dimmock, Ole Devil intended to
take revenge personally. So Tommy concentrated on loading
and drawing his bow to deal with the second man.

Studying the hesitant behavior of all but the leading pair of
Dragoons, the Oriental decided that the use of the *wata-kusi*
points the previous evening was paying dividends. Unfortunately he had brought only the two of them with him. Nor had

he any more of the *hiki-ya* heads, not that he contemplated employing another one under the present circumstances.

Having straight edges and being diamond-shaped in section, the *yanagi-ha*—"willow leaf"—point lacked the specialized qualities of the other types of heads, but that did not detract from its worth.[1] It was the most efficient general-purpose point used by the *kyudoka*. Such was the kind of arrow upon which he was now relying.

Sighting in the traditional *yami*, "eclipse" fashion, so that the stave of the bow covered the center of the target, Tommy loosed the arrow as soon as he heard the flat crack of Ole Devil's rifle. Shot in the head with a .45-caliber bullet, the sergeant went backward over the cantle of his saddle. Flying somewhat slower, the arrow still arrived with sufficient velocity to pierce the Dragoon's breastplate and reach the vital organs it was supposed to protect. Dropping the saber with a shriek of mortal torment, he grabbed at the shaft that was protruding from his chest and tumbled, dying, off his horse.

Thumbing down the catch at the right side of the rifle's frame, Ole Devil caused the simple mechanism to operate. The slide magazine crawled through the aperture until the next loaded chamber was in line with the bore and was crammed forward against the opening. Then, without taking the butt from his shoulder, he reached with his forefinger to draw down the underhammer. In far less time than was possible with any contemporary single-barreled firearm, he was ready to shoot again.

As quickly as the Texian was able to recharge the piece, Tommy could replenish his more primitive weapon with even greater rapidity. Gathering up the third arrow, he nocked it to the string. However, he did not make his draw immediately. None of the other Dragoons were as near as the first pair, and he had no wish to waste a shaft. He had been fortunate in felling his man at that range, and anywhere beyond it would

1. The *yanagi-ha* corresponds with such utilitarian Occidental arrow points as the Bear 4-Blade Razorheads, described in the "Bunduki" series.— J.T.E.

almost certainly see the arrow repelled by the metal breastplate, which might give the soldiers encouragement to press home an attack.

Ole Devil had no such inhibitions. Sighting, he fired and saw the man at whom he had aimed reel under the impact, although he did not fall. Instead he reined his horse around and sent it at a gallop in the direction from which he had come. Panic of that kind was generally infectious, and so it proved on this occasion. Without the presence of either Almonte or the sergeant to make them continue the attack upon what—if the number of horses to be seen was any guide—appeared to be several of the enemy, the rest of the Dragoons also turned and took their departure.

"We've done it, Devil-san," Tommy said with satisfaction, lowering the bow and returning the *yanagi-ha* shaft to his quiver. "Shall I go and make sure that no more of them are coming?"

"Yes," Ole Devil replied, looking at the Oriental in a speculative manner. "Do that."

Giving the Texian no chance to ask the questions he knew would be forthcoming, Tommy went to collect the dead vaquero's horse that he had been using. He was not ashamed of the decisions he had made where Paul Dimmock was concerned, but there were more important things to do at that moment than discuss them.

Riding toward the top of the ridge, Tommy stopped before he reached the edge. Dismounting and allowing the animal to stand ground hitched, he advanced the remaining distance on foot until he could see over without allowing himself to be seen in return. As he expected, the party of Dragoons was still riding downward and showed no sign of turning back. Nor were any more of the enemy making the ascent. On the trail, looking like a disturbed ants' nest with various of its personnel milling around, the column had come to a halt, and several officers were making their way in the direction of the advance party.

There was, however, something of vastly greater interest and significance for the Oriental to observe. Some short distance from the remainder of the Dragoons' bodyguard and on foot,

Presidente Antonio Lopez de Santa Anna was surrounded by a group composed of his dinner guests from the previous evening. Among them, the center of all their attention, was Colonel Juan Almonte displaying a sheet of paper and holding several more in his hand. Standing nearby, Dimmock's horse supplied the clue to what was happening.

Clearly the "reward posters" and the "government's" letter, which the lieutenant should have dropped "accidentally" with his saddlebags while ascending the slope, had reached their destination in a much more convincing manner. Everything now depended on whether *el Presidente* would accept them at their face value and act upon them in the way that Major General Samuel Houston hoped.

Deciding that there was nothing more he could see or do at that time, Tommy stood for a moment with his feet together and hands clenched by his side. He bowed at the waist toward the body of his dead companion in a silent and respectful salutation. Then, picking up the bow that he had laid down so as to pay his tribute to Dimmock, he withdrew from his point of vantage. Retrieving the *hiki-ya* and *yanagi-ha* arrows in passing, the latter being far easier than a *wata-kusi* point to remove from the body of its victim, he rejoined his employer. As they started to ride eastward, he reported all he had seen and deduced.

"You're probably right about them being more likely to be convinced by the posters and letters after the way they fell into their hands," Ole Devil conceded bitterly when the Oriental had finished speaking. Studying the inscrutable mask of the other's face, he went on, "Did Paul tell you what he intended to do?"

"No," Tommy replied.

"When did you guess?" the Texian challenged.

"Watching him last night, I thought he might be considering something of the sort," Tommy admitted, with none of the mock-deferential manner he adopted in more relaxed moments or when he felt there was need to relieve his companions' tensions. "Twice before I left my home, I saw samurai who were

dishonored and under the obligation to commit seppuku.[2] Each
time he looked and behaved as Dimmock-san was doing."

"Paul wasn't dishonored," Ole Devil protested. "It was just
the opposite in fact."

"We knew that," Tommy replied, "but *he* believed he was."

"Then why didn't you say something to me instead of letting
him go through with it?" Ole Devil demanded savagely, as
close as he had ever come to being furious with his loyal little
companion.

"How a man chooses to live or to die is his own right, Devil-
san," Tommy answered with quiet dignity and gentleness. "It is
not for others, even his friends, to interfere. Dimmock-san believed that for the rest of his life, even though he had been on
this mission, he would live under a dark cloud because of his
flight from Goliad. Always there would be those who sought to
remind him—and his parents too—that he was still alive when
many of his comrades-in-arms were killed. Sooner or later it
would come that he either had to kill somebody or be killed
himself. So he thought it was preferable to die now, usefully
and with honor. If I had doubted him, I would have spoken."

"I know you would, *amigo,*" Ole Devil admitted, nodding
his approval. Then he gave a sigh and went on, "He died usefully and with honor, all right." His voice dropped to little
more than a whisper, yet throbbed with emotion as he concluded, "You crazy, gallant fool, Paul. By the good Lord, I'll
do everything I can to make sure that you haven't died in
vain."

Lieutenant Paul Dimmock could have asked for no better
assurance, nor epitaph!

* * *

2. *Seppuku:* "disembowelment," a ritual suicide, also vulgarly called *hari-
kiri,* "belly-slitting." If a *samurai* transgressed in certain ways against the
code of *Bushido,* he was under an obligation to take his own life and usually
did this by a ritualized form of disembowelment. The reason Tommy Okasi
had to leave Japan did not fall into such a category. See footnote 2, Appendix B.—J.T.E.

Colonel Juan Almonte was waiting with what little patience he could muster for the man he had sent after the dead gringo's horse to return. A glance at the trail had informed him that Ramón Caro had quit the box of the leading baggage wagon and was joining their superior. He could trust that dirty little rat of a letter-scribbler to try and put him in a bad light over the shooting, and he wanted to refute such a claim as quickly as possible.

Watching the pursuers ascending the slope, the colonel scowled as he noticed that they were not attempting to duplicate the little "Indian's" speed. Without sympathizing, as he was not personally endangered, he knew why they were holding back. Deciding that bellowing for them to hurry would do more harm than good by drawing attention to their reluctance to carry out a duty of such importance, he walked over to inspect the gringo's body. He drew no conclusions, other than that Dimmock was a Texian and had been party to a plot to assassinate *el Presidente* that had failed at each attempt. The arrival of the Dragoon with the horse saved him from the need to conduct a closer examination.

"Search him," Almonte barked, taking the animal's reins. "Bring me any papers he has."

On the point of mounting the horse, the colonel noticed that the right-side saddlebag was open and that something white showed from within. Failing to notice that the bags were not secured to the rig in the usual way, more out of curiosity than for any other reason, he lifted the flap and pulled forth the sheaf of papers. One glance drove all thoughts of anything else from his head. The top sheet's message was not written in his native tongue, but he could both speak and read English with considerable fluency.

"Madre de Dios!" Almonte croaked as he read the printed words, then he looked at the second sheet.

"What is it, señor?" asked the Dragoon who was kneeling by the corpse, gazing at his superior in alarm as the discovery of the paper's inscription elicited an even more violent and profane remark.

"Mind your own damned business!" Almonte thundered,

and the man cowered before his obvious rage. "Has that carrion any papers on it?"

"I—I haven't found any yet, *patrón,*" the Dragoon replied.

"Then keep looking until you do," the colonel ordered, thrusting back all but the top two sheets of paper and swinging astride the horse. "If there are any, bring them straight to me. Don't read them—"

"I—I can't read, señor," the alarmed soldier confessed.

"So much the better—for you," Almonte said grimly. "Make sure that nobody else sees them—*nobody* at all, understand?"

"*Sí, señor,*" assented the Dragoon, returning to his task and wondering what had been on the papers to cause his superior such consternation.

Deciding that it was none of his business and that he might even find it ill advised to pry, the Dragoon appropriated Dimmock's knife as his loot. Promising himself that he would also try to lay claim to at least one of the gringo's pistols, he went on with what proved to be a profitless task. The Texian had no documents on his person, nor anything else that could have identified him.

Riding toward where Santa Anna had dismounted, Almonte noted without surprise or pleasure that—as was only to be expected—the rest of the staff were assembling. Galloping from where he had been leading the main body of the column, General Vincente Filisola almost flung himself from his saddle in a manner vastly different from his normally stodgy movements. Colonel Ricardo Dromundo had quit *el President*'s carriage, in which he had been riding, and was already on the scene. All the rest of the previous night's dinner guests, equally curious, were also there or coming fast so as to find out what had happened.

"We've got the gringo who shot at you, Your Excellency," the colonel reported unnecessarily, conscious of the way the others were scrutinizing him, as he swung to the ground and kept hold of the horse's reins. "My men are after the 'Indian.' "

"I hope *they* have enough sense to take *him* alive," Caro put in. "His Excellency wants prisoners to question, not corpses."

"There's something I must show you, Your Excellency," Almonte continued, paying no attention to the comment beyond scowling at its maker. "But it should be for your eyes only."

"What is it?" Santa Anna demanded impatiently, glancing at the papers in the colonel's hands and impressed, in spite of the annoyance aroused by Caro's reminder, by his air of urgency.

"The less who know of these, the better, Your Excellency," Almonte warned, who shared the entire staff's knowledge that *el Presidente* expected the honorific to be used every time he was addressed. Making a small gesture with the documents, but preventing their contents from being read, he hinted, "Shall I send my men away?"

"Tell them to go and wait by my carriage," Santa Anna instructed, his curiosity making him more amenable than he would otherwise have been.

While Almonte could dismiss the men under his command to a safe distance, he had no such authority over his fellow members of the staff. Nor, being bitter rivals and none trusting any of the others, were they willing to be excluded from a discovery that was obviously of considerable importance. So Filisola and the rest gathered closer as the Dragoons retired. Wanting to avoid dissension by appearing to make favorites, *el Presidente* allowed them to remain.

Although the group pretended to dismiss the "reward posters", which Almonte—ever the showman—exhibited first, their attitudes were much as Lieutenant Carlos Catañeda y Abamillo of the Zacatecas Lancers had been when Ole Devil Hardin had allowed him to read one. What was more, being closer to the source, they had better cause to duplicate the young officer's summation of what might happen if such a proposal was presented to the members of the column. All of them realized, although none would have been foolish enough to admit it openly, that Santa Anna was far from being the popular and well-loved leader to which he laid claim. There were enlisted men, officers even, to whom the chance of gaining such a large reward might have considerable appeal.

"So they offer to pay a bounty for me," Santa Anna sniffed, but he, too, was displaying a not-too-well-concealed apprehension. He waved a hand toward the poster that the colonel had exhibited. "Even if they had posted those things, nobody would have taken the offer seriously."

"Except that, as Your Excellency knows, *somebody* already has," Almonte pointed out, not averse to capitalizing on his superior's dilemma. *"Twice!"*

"Who?" el Presidente demanded, surveying the members of his staff with considerable and, under the circumstances, unjustified, suspicion.

"The two men who have already tried to kill you," the colonel explained, ignoring his colleagues' antagonistic glares although delighted to have scored such a point against them.

"The two—!" Caro snorted derisively, falling even deeper into the trap. "One was a Texian and the other an 'Indian.' They had . . ."

"Had been sent by the land thieves' so-called *government* to deliver the posters to our soldiers," Almonte finished when the secretary's words trailed away due to a realization that they might be injudicious. "Only that might not have been all they were told to do. They might have had another purpose too."

"And what might *that* have been, Juan?" Santa Anna inquired, almost mildly for him.

"To assassinate Your Excellency themselves," Almonte explained, noticing the use of his Christian name with satisfaction. "If they had succeeded, the reward would be given to them. Even if they were killed trying, their leaders were confident that the posters would be found and distributed among our men."

"That's true," Filisola conceded before he could stop himself.

"They wouldn't do such a thing!" Caro protested, as the colonel had hoped he would.

"Why not, if they were authorized to do it and indemnified against the consequences?" Almonte challenged, grinning savagely at the secretary before making his face respectful and offering his superior—he counted only *el Presidente* in that category—the other sheet of paper. "As Your Excellency will see from *this.*"

Accepting the document, Santa Anna stared at it for several

seconds. His eyes went along the printed lines and his lips worked soundlessly as he mouthed the more lengthy and difficult words. Although he spoke English passably, he was less familiar with the language in its written, or even printed, form. For all that, his breathing turned to deep, almost snorting, grunts, and his florid cheeks became suffused with blood as he realized what the message implied.

From what *el Presidente* was able to deduce, he was reading an authorization for the bearer of the document to kill him by, to quote, *"whatever means or methods are most convenient, the more painful and lingering the better, as befitting a tyrant and a cold-blooded murderer whose death will benefit all mankind, including the down-trodden and ill-used Mexican soldiers he is wantonly sending to their death."* There followed a far more accurate estimate of the casualties suffered by his army during the siege at the Alamo Mission than he had allowed to be published in Mexico.[3] It was printed on the official stationery of the so-called Republic of Texas, copies of which he had already received from his spies, and was apparently signed by "President" David G. Burnet, who was reported to have supplanted the former "Governor," Henry Smith.

"What is it, may one ask, Your Excellency?" Caro said, puzzled by the expression of malevolence and alarm that had come to his employer's face.

"Take a look at this!" Santa Anna commanded, so overcome by wrath and concern that he passed the document to his secretary without a moment's hesitation. "Those 'land thief' swine are trying to have me assassinated!"

"It is as *I* said, Your Excellency," Almonte commented, hiding under an aura of commiseration, his satisfaction at having had his judgment of the situation's gravity confirmed. "They know that with *you* dead, we are without a leader—"

"What does it say?" Filisola demanded of Caro, before the colonel's platitude could be completed.

---

3. According to *Presidente* Santa Anna's official communiqué, over six hundred Texians were killed at a cost of "about" seventy Mexicans dead and three hundred wounded.—J.T.E.

"However, there's no proof that it's genuine," the secretary concluded, having translated the contents of the document for the benefit of the other members of the staff. He refused to admit that he did not doubt its authenticity because of his greatest rival's contribution to its delivery. "I've never seen Burnet's signa—"

The ploy failed miserably!

"Genuine?" Santa Anna bellowed, before Almonte in particular could express a refutation of the secretary's statement. He knew that while he would not have been so indiscreet as to put them into writing, the orders and the indemnification of their bearer against any legal consequences were such as he would have given. "Of course it's genuine!" He glared around furiously, continuing, "Do you think any of that foreign scum would be willing to let themselves be killed just to convince me that a forgery is genuine?"

"Only a man who is devoted to *you* would make such a sacrifice, Your Excellency," Almonte declared, and seeing an opportunity to make yet another display of their loyalty,[4] the rest of the staff muttered sycophantic concurrence. "So that damnable document *must* be genuine."

"It's genuine, all right!" Santa Anna said, gritting his teeth.

"What do you intend to do about it, Your Excellency?" Filisola inquired respectfully, being aware that *el Presidente* invariably dictated every aspect of policy personally and without consulting anybody else.

"Do?" Santa Anna almost shrieked, crushing the paper as if wishing to choke the hateful words from it. *"Do?* Those swine want me killed, do they? Well they're going to have a chance to earn their blood money themselves. We're marching to this 'temporary capital' of theirs as fast as we can move."

4. During the final assault on the Alamo Mission, General Manuel Fernandez Castrillón showed hesitation when *Presidente* Santa Anna ordered him to shoot six prisoners who were taken. Wishing to demonstrate their devotion to duty, the members of *el Presidente's* staff—who had taken no part in the actual fighting—drew their swords and carried out the "executions" with such vigor that they almost included Castrillón among their victims. —J.T.E.

"To Harrisburg?" Filisola asked, remembering from the reports that had been received that the Republic of Texas's Army were traveling far to the northeast of that town. "But what of Houston and his men, Your Excellency?"

"Them?" el Presidente snarled, intolerant as always of any question being put regarding his decisions. "What are they? A disorganized and cowardly rabble in full flight from us and unworthy of our attention. No, gentlemen, it is the head of this treacherous and perfidious snake we must remove. We are marching to Harrisburg with all speed."

15

HOT DAMN, WE'LL OBLIGE YOU!

"Santa Anna's taken the bait, all right, sir," Ole Devil Hardin reported. "He's marching for Harrisburg with such haste that, with the exception of a single six-pounder, he's left all his artillery behind with the baggage train, and he's driving his men so hard that they're dropping out by the dozen. They'd just arrived at Thompson's Ferry and were starting to cross the river when we were relieved by Colonel Smith. But, for all his losses along the way, he still has us outnumbered by at least three to one."

The time was just before eleven o'clock on the morning of April 13.

In spite of his obvious fatigue the young Texian was standing almost as rigidly while at ease as he had been at attention before receiving Major General Samuel Houston's permission to relax. He had refused the offer of a chair, knowing that he was so tired from the exertion of the past few days if he sat down, he might fall asleep before he had informed his superior officer of what had happened.

Having kept *Presidente* Antonio Lopez de Santa Anna's column under observation and making sure of the direction in which it was marching, until the meeting with "Deaf" Smith on the banks of the Brazos River had relieved him of the necessity, Ole Devil was able to announce that his mission was showing every sign of having been successful. Goaded by what he had regarded as two murderous attempts on his life—once with a weapon calculated to doom him to a lingering death—and reading the contents of the documents that Lieutenant Paul Dimmock's act of self-sacrifice had put into his possession, the Mexican dictator was behaving as Houston had hoped he would.

Contrary to *el Presidente*'s supposition, his assailants had never intended to kill or even wound him.

To have done either would not have produced the results General Houston desired!

There were generals far more competent and active than Vincente Filisola in Santa Anna's column, and whichever of them had assumed command after Santa Anna's death, he would almost certainly have followed the tactically sound course of continuing to pursue the Republic of Texas's Army. Destroying or scattering it would achieve far more useful results than killing the members of the "foreign land thieves" government.

Only Santa Anna himself would have such a deep personal involvement that he would wish, to the exclusion of everything else, to wreak vengeance upon the men he believed to be responsible for the two attempts to murder him. By doing so, he was playing into General Houston's hands. Not only was the latter being granted a desperately needed respite, but the wild dash to Harrisburg was weakening the already dispirited force under *el Presidente*'s command.

The respite was a very important consideration for the commanding general of the Republic of Texas's Army under the conditions that were currently prevailing.

For all the cries of outrage that had arisen over the fate of the Alamo Mission's defenders, there had been no significant increase in the numbers of their fellow Texians to volunteer for service with the army. In fact, as the reports of the "Runaway

Scrape"[1] and the successes of General José Urrea's Tamaulipa
Brigade at San Patricio and Goliad began to circulate, many of
those who had already enlisted deserted with the intention of
protecting and removing their families beyond the enemies'
reach.

Even the hard core of staunch men who had remained under
Houston's command, barely a thousand in all, were unhappy
over the way he was conducting the campaign. Since the majority of them had been armed with the consignment of caplock
rifles Lieutenant Mannen Blaze had had awaiting their arrival
at Groce's Place, there had been increasing demands that they
should "quit running and make a stab at getting even for what
had happened to those gallant boys of the Alamo." So far the
general had been able to fend them off by insisting that the
army learned the ways of the new weapons. However, knowing
the mood the men were in, he was aware that he could not
restrain their impatience indefinitely. Something positive would
have to be done before long.

Unfortunately, as Houston appreciated, the action he must
take next would not be popular.

"I hear you lost young Dimmock," the general said.

"Yes, sir," Ole Devil agreed, his face taking on angry and
bitter lines as he explained the circumstances of the lieutenant's
death. "That was what convinced Santa Anna the 'reward posters' and 'President Burnet's' letter were genuine," he concluded. "But I didn't know what P—Mr. Dimmock had in
mind—"

"*That* goes without saying, Captain," Houston declared.
"And, as soon as it's possible, we'll let it be known what he
did."[2]

---

1. In General Houston's opinion, the "Runaway Scrape" had a worse effect
on morale than any of the misfortunes that had befallen the Texians. He
informed the government via its secretary of war, "Your removal to Harrisburg has done more to increase the panic in the country than anything else
that has occurred in Texas, except the fall of the Alamo."—J.T.E.

2. Unfortunately, for political reasons, Major General Houston was advised
to make no reference to the trick that had been played on *Presidente* Santa
Anna. So neither Ole Devil Hardin nor Lieutenant Dimmock could be

"Thank you, sir," Ole Devil drawled, fighting to hold off a yawn.

"And now, my young friend," Houston went on, rising. "I'm ordering you to go and sleep. You look like you're ready for it."

"I am," Ole Devil admitted, but he still snapped smartly to attention before continuing. "Can you tell me when we'll be moving out, please, sir?"

"I'll have the *Yellow Stone* start ferrying the men over this afternoon," Houston replied, referring to a little steamboat that had traded along the Brazos River before the beginning of hostilities and that had already played one important part in the campaign.[3] Your company will be the last to go, which means they'll be here until tomorrow. So you'll be able to have a good rest."

"*Gracias,* sir," Ole Devil said.

"Now, get going, blast you," the general barked, but there was a kindly and even admiring glint in his blue eyes to belie the gruffness of his voice. "I've work to do, whether you young line officers have or not."

Leaving Houston's headquarters, Ole Devil did not go straight to bed. Instead he accompanied Mannen Blaze to a secluded area. In a small canvas shelter, a bathtub—"borrowed" from its original owner—was filled with hot water and awaiting him. Removing his clothes for the first time since setting out on the mission, he took a bath, shaved and trimmed his beard and mustache to their normal style, then donned his uniform. As a further demonstration of the respect and high regard in which the men of the Texas Light Cavalry's Company C held him, they had set up a tent well clear of the noise and bustle of the main camp. They also willingly formed a ring of sentries to ensure that he and Tommy Okasi, who had already bathed and changed, could sleep undisturbed.

* * *

given the credit they deserved. All that could be said was the latter had died showing great courage during a patrol that encountered a large body of Mexican soldiers.—J.T.E.

3. How is told in *Ole Devil and the Mule Train.*—J.T.E.

"Devil!" Mannen Blaze said urgently, shaking his cousin's shoulder.

"Wh—!" Ole Devil gasped, waking up far more slowly than was usual for him. "Wh—What is it?"

"I'm sorry to have to disturb you," the burly redhead said apologetically, sounding as if he, too, was practically asleep. "But there could be trouble."

Swinging his feet from the cot, which like the bathtub had been "borrowed" by the men of Company C, Ole Devil saw that Tommy was also stirring. The Oriental had removed the stain and, except that his face was a little drawn after the exertions of the past few days, looked his usual self. There was a muted rumble of conversation from not far outside the tent and, looking through the open flaps, the Texian could tell that the afternoon was well advanced. He had slept long enough to have lost the fatigue that had assailed him and felt much refreshed.

"What kind of trouble?" Ole Devil inquired as he stood up.

"There's a meeting of protest, they call it, going on," Mannen explained, his sleepy tones underlaid with anger. "Some of the anti-Houston bunch are trying to talk the others into heading straight down to Thompson's Ferry and jump Santa Anna instead of what they call running like cur dogs with our tails between our legs."

"They're *what?*" Ole Devil barked, bending down to collect his belt and passing its end through the first loop on the left side of his breeches. Although he slid on the bowie knife's sheath, he did not bother to replace the magazine pouch, both of which he had removed when extracting the belt from his trousers. Encircling his waist with it, he fastened the buckle and pulled on his boots, asking savagely, "Haven't the damned fools been told what General Houston's going to do?"

"Only that we're crossing the Brazos and moving east," Mannen replied, gesturing angrily with his cousin's Manton pistol—which he had taken away and cleaned—looking almost tiny in his huge right hand.

"Of course," Ole Devil said quietly, slipping the bowie knife into its sheath. "He can't let it be known what he's intending.

There's still time for word of it to get to Santa Anna and spoil every chance of it working."

"It's a pity he couldn't let folks know, though," the redhead stated, handing over the pistol. "What started the fuss is that some Mexican sneaked up close enough to the camp so that he could shout that *el Presidente* knows we're skulking in the bushes up here and that after he's whipped our 'land thieves' government out of the country, he'll be coming to smoke us out for the cowardly rats we are."

"So they want to go down there and call his bluff?" Ole Devil guessed, accepting and thrusting his pistol into its carrier on the belt.

"They reckon that, seeing they've got those new caplocks, they should use them for shooting," Mannen elaborated, "not as extra ballast while they're running away."

"God-damned fools!" Ole Devil growled. "Can't they see that Santa Anna sent his man up here to try to make us go there? He'll have left enough men at Thompson's to take care of us, and if we go there, we'll be playing into his hands."[4]

"It's likely never occurred to them," the redhead answered, having drawn a similar conclusion. "Somebody ought to tell them."

"Where's General Houston?" Ole Devil demanded.

"He took all the senior officers across the river in the *Yellow Stone,*" Mannen replied. "That's when those stupid sons of bitches started stirring the others up."

"They've got to be stopped before they do it," Ole Devil declared in a voice barely louder than a whisper. He raised it to go on, "And, by God, I'm going to." His next words were more of a statement than a question. "Is the company formed up, Mr. Blaze?"

"*Armed* and waiting, sir," Mannen reported, showing no re-

---

4. Ole Devil Hardin's summation was correct. *Presidente* Santa Anna had left General Ramirez Sesma and a thousand men at Thompson's Ferry, hoping to trap the Republic of Texas's Army between them and the force led by General Vincente Filisola, which was escorting the baggage train, if they responded to his insulting message.—J.T.E.

sentiment at the use of the honorific *mister*. He had anticipated his cousin's response and made all the necessary arrangements. "As soon as you're ready, sir, we can move out."

While the conversation was taking place, Tommy had risen and armed himself with his *daisho*. Deciding that the bow would not be required, he left it on the ground and held out his employer's hat. Taking it, Ole Devil did not put it on his head. Instead he allowed it to dangle over his back by the *barbiquejo* chinstrap.

As their commanding officer stepped from the tent, Sergeant Smith called the two ranks of Company C to attention. Studying the expectancy and resolution on the tanned faces of his men, Ole Devil knew he could rely upon them to back him to the hilt. Returning the salute that Smith delivered, he gave the order to turn right and led the way to where a certain amount of noise indicated the meeting was taking place.

Studying the crowd which had gathered on an area of open ground at the fringes of the camp, Ole Devil found it to be comprised exactly as he had expected. Mostly they were just ordinary enlisted men, not overly intelligent and unable to appreciate the true nature of the situation. There were also a few malcontents with real or fancied grievances and an assortment of the kind who would go along anywhere that something was happening, regardless of what it might be. As Mannen had said, the main causes of the dissension were the sprinkling of men who were opposed to General Houston and wanted to discredit him.

However, although the meeting had been going on for several minutes, it was clear to Ole Devil that no decision had been reached. Either no leader had arisen with sufficient strength of personality to dominate the group or no member of the anti-Houston faction was willing to accept the responsibility personally.

All eyes turned toward Company C as they approached and the rumble of conversation died away. There was not a man present who was unacquainted with Ole Devil, although he could not recognize any whom he could claim as friends or associates. One thing he did know, they were all aware that his sympathies were definitely pro-Houston, and they could probably guess why he had come.

When some fifty yards separated them from the crowd, Sergeant Smith gave an order, and displaying a military precision only rarely seen in the Republic of Texas's Army, the two files of Company C fanned out. They halted in a double file, so positioned that the men in front were not in line of fire of those at the rear, behind the human triangle formed by Tommy Okasi, Ole Devil, and Mannen Blaze.

"Well, *gentlemen,*" Ole Devil said, standing ramrod straight in front of his company and sweeping the crowd with a cold gaze. "What's all this about?"

"Us fellers're quick sick of running," answered the burly man in the forefront of the gathering, looking distinctly uneasy at finding himself apparently being singled out to act as their spokesman. "So we, *all of us,* conclude it's time we did something else."

"Don't you think General Houston's doing it?" Ole Devil challenged.

"Sure he is," scoffed a speaker who was careful to keep himself concealed among the crowd when the burly man did not reply—nor anybody else—for several seconds. "He-all's aiming to do the same's he's been doing all along. Keep running away!"

Listening to the muted, so-far-anything-but-unanimous mutter of agreement, Ole Devil was hard put to control his temper. Yet he knew to lose it would be ruinous. Unless he handled the situation correctly, he would ruin all his mission had achieved, and Paul Dimmock's self-sacrifice would have been made in vain.

The latter consideration, even more than Ole Devil's sense of duty—which would have compelled him to intervene at the meeting anyway—made him determined to prevent the crowd from carrying out their intentions. If they did, it was almost certain that the majority of the army—already furious and eager to avenge the slaughter of the Alamo Mission's defenders and the massacre at Goliad—would insist upon accompanying them.

So, although Dimmock's death was a great inducement to succeed, Ole Devil knew that it must not be allowed to cloud his judgment and lead him into a rashness that would have disastrous consequences.

The situation was, Ole Devil realized, very similar to the one he had faced on leaving the hollow at San Felipe after the duel.

There was, however, one vitally important difference.

This time Ole Devil could not count upon the assistance of friends who appreciated the situation and were mingling with the opposition so as to help him. Lacking such an asset, he would have to rely upon his own knowledge of human nature and—although he had never heard of the word—crowd, or mob, psychology.

Studying the attitudes and expressions of the crowd, the young captain forced himself to control his growing anger. Instead he drew his conclusions in the deliberate and calculating fashion that made him such a deadly efficient fighting man and an extremely capable leader.

While the group might have congregated, they were as yet far from being united in their purpose. Nor, which was even more important, had any one of them displayed the cool and forceful kind of personality that was needed to direct their efforts. Unless one did, backed as he was by his grim-faced, loyal, and resolute company, Ole Devil believed that he could disperse them.

"And what do *you* say should be done?" the young captain demanded, still addressing the person he had apparently decided was the leader of the crowd.

"Me?" came the indignant and not unexpected reply. "I just aim to do what the rest of these fellers want to do."

"And we aims to have us a fight, is what!" declared the second speaker, still without allowing himself to be identified.

"That's what General Houston intends to give you," Ole Devil pointed out. "But it will be when he and not Santa Anna wants it."

"When'll that be?" demanded the voice from somewhere in the center of the crowd. "After Santa Anna's growed too old to fight back?"

"Go and draw a line between us, Tommy," Ole Devil said quietly, then spoke louder. "It will be soon, and when it comes, we'll have the best chance of licking Santa Anna that anybody could want."

Silence fell after the captain had made the statement, and every eye followed the Oriental's movements. Advancing until he was halfway between the two groups, he employed *laijitsu* to whip out the *tachi*. Without as much as a glance at the puzzled onlookers, he obeyed his employer's instructions. Having done so, he replaced the sword just as quickly and returned to his position in front of Company C.

"All right!" Ole Devil went on, his savage scrutiny raking the faces of the crowd. "Are you willing to let General Houston pick the time and place for us to tackle Santa Anna?"

"Like hell we are!" yelled the man from the midst of the gathering. Although there was little obvious support for his sentiments, he went on. "We aim to have us a fight right now, and that's what we're going to do."

"Very well!" Ole Devil barked, pointing at the groove carved by Tommy Okasi's sword. "If all you want is to fight for the sake of it, hot damn, we'll oblige you! Anybody who's so inclined, walk over that line—but be ready to start shooting as soon as you're across."

A good two hundred strong, as opposed to at the most forty-five men behind their challenger, the dissidents still stood indecisive and exchanged glances. They all knew the members of the Texas Light Cavalry's hard-riding, harder-fighting Company C would not hesitate to carry out *any* command given by the satanic-faced young captain. Nor would they be influenced by the fact that they were confronting fellow Texians.

So every dissident was waiting for somebody else to guide him!

Each knew that whoever crossed the line would have a fight to the death on his hands. There was a sudden, concerted sucking in of breath as a man stepped forward.

Watching the tall, long-haired, unkempt, and buckskin-clad figure approaching, not a sign of apprehension showed on Ole Devil's Mephistophelian features. For all that, he was consumed by anxiety. It seemed that his challenge was being accepted.

Once the man reached the line, others were sure to follow him!

When that happened, a situation could erupt that was going to end the Republic of Texas's small army as a fighting force.

With a bitter and sinking sensation in the pit of his stomach, Ole Devil told himself that his gamble was not producing the desired results. Behind him the men of Company C stood like statues. Yet nobody who looked at them could fail to appreciate their readiness to take whatever kind of action might become necessary. Their very stillness, caused by the instructions he had given as they were marching to the meeting, was impressive and the crowd had taken notice of it. So he had felt sure that, confronted by such a disciplined body of grimly determined and well-armed men, nobody in the gathering would be willing to take the initiative against them.

That one should have could be disastrous.

However, there was one slight consolation for the young Texian: As yet, nobody else was moving forward! Clearly the rest of the crowd were waiting to find out what happened when the man crossed the line.

There was, Ole Devil decided, only one chance of averting a full-scale clash.

If the buckskin-clad man could be killed swiftly, unexpectedly, and without any suggestion of hesitation the moment he crossed the line, his companions might have second thoughts about following.

Using the techniques for drawing and firing the Manton pistol that he had developed, Ole Devil was confident that he could do it.

However, the young Texian also appreciated the dangers of such an act. There was a possibility that the crowd would feel called upon to avenge their self-appointed leader.

Yet, to yield and let the man cross would weld the onlookers into a united band against which no kind of verbal argument would prevail.

It was, Ole Devil knew, always best to take a positive action in such conditions—even if to do so meant taking the life of a brave, if misguided, man!

From his position to the right and rear, Mannen Blaze could not see his cousin's face. For all that, he could guess at the way Ole Devil was thinking. Remembering what was at stake and also how Paul Dimmock had willingly given his life to bring it about, Ole Devil was in the state of mind when he was at his most ruthless and dangerous.

In the redhead's opinion, the life expectancy of the advancing man was no longer than it would take for him to walk four more paces. The moment his foot passed over the line drawn by Tommy, in the hope that the suddenness of his death would dissuade the others, Ole Devil would kill him in his tracks.

There was no other way to deal with the situation! Not with the future of the Republic of Texas in the balance. Nor after Paul Dimmock had allowed himself to be killed to bring about the state of affairs that the crowd's wish to march south was threatening.

In the next few seconds the fate of all they had been striving for would be resolved—one way or the other!

"I'm coming over there, Cap'n Hardin, sir," the potential leader announced in carrying tones that, despite having a somewhat different timbre, reminded Ole Devil of the unknown agitator's voice. "And *I* ain't like *some* 's's a-scared to show themselves when they talking big about wanting to fight."

For all the employment of the honorific *sir,* the young Texian decided that the words had an undesirable import. Obviously the speaker had the kind of nature that must accept *any* challenge. Furthermore, his comment suggested that he could not be the agitator who had remained incognito among their colleagues.

"I told you how it is if you come across," Ole Devil said in flat and dispassionate tones, making the words sound more of an unavoidable fact rather than a threat or a warning. "So, on your own head be it if you do."

"I'm coming over, Cap'n," the man repeated.

A silence that could almost be felt had come over the crowd.

Every eye was fixed upon Ole Devil and his challenger to the exclusion of all else.

At the most, two more steps would see the latter crossing the line!

Standing motionless, but with his satanic face as implacable as fate, Ole Devil was getting set to bring free and discharge the Manton pistol!

The man stopped a good stride clear of the dividing mark. "Only not to take you up on it, sir," he went on as a sighing gasp arose from the crowd and the members of Company C alike. "No, sir, Cap'n Hardin. By grab, you're right in what you said, and I'll be honored to stand alongside you on it."

"And I'm with you, mister!" called a voice to which excitement, or some other emotion, had given a timbre closer to a contralto than a tenor. "We'll get all the fighting we want when General Houston knows the time's right for it. So, by cracky, that's good enough for me."

For all the somewhat effeminate tones, the figure that stepped forward was very masculine in appearance. Not that, with the wide-brimmed black hat on his head and a luxuriant mass of bushy black whiskers, much could be seen of his features. Buttoned to the neck, a heavy black cloak-coat obscured him to the top of his riding boots, and his hands were buried in its pockets.

"And for me," seconded the man in the buckskins. "We ain't scared of 'em none, but we all know just how big an army Santa Anna's got. Say what you will about Sam Houston, he is neither a fool nor a coward. If he don't want to lock horns with 'em, it's 'cause he knows the time 'n' place ain't right. When it be, he'll be out there ahead and leading us." He darted a scathing look over his shoulder at the crowd. "Not staying hid like some when they're making big talk about wanting to fight and gets offered the chance. Be it all right if I step up and join you, Cap'n Hardin?"

"I'd be proud to have you, sir," Ole Devil answered. "And anybody else who has the true interests of Texas at heart."

Even as he was speaking, the Texian wondered where he had seen the other man before. There was something vaguely familiar about the grimy and unshaven face. He also wished that his supporter had selected the words of the speech with greater care. The latter part of them had constituted a direct challenge to the agitator. Fortunately that worthy did not offer to put in an appearance.

"That's me, for one," the smaller figure declared, following the other man across the line. "Who'll else's with us?"

"Take the company back to our lines, Mr. Blaze!" Ole Devil ordered, without waiting to see what the response would be. "They've plenty to do before General Houston marches us out."

Given that much of a lead from two of their number and a gesture of peace by the young captain, particularly as the agitator in their midst had not advanced to refute the references to his desire for anonymity, the rest of the gathering began to reconsider the justice of its purpose. All had heard of how large a force Santa Anna had at his disposal and realized that, new caplocks or not, they would be greatly outnumbered. Nor could any of them, even his antagonists, truthfully argue against the remark regarding General Houston's courage and sagacity. Wise in the ways of waging war, he could be counted on to know how best to cope with an enemy of such overwhelming strength.

"Hey!" called one of the crowd. "The *Yellow Stone*'s coming back."

"Come on, Billy," another said to his neighbor. "Our outfit's due to go aboard her. Let's get back so's we'll be ready to go."

Once somebody had made the first move to depart, the crowd dissolved like grains of sand scattered by the wind. Seeing that they had failed to make their point, the anti-Houston faction did not attempt to stop the rest. Soon only Ole Devil and his two supporters remained.

"Egad, my Mephistophelian young friend," said the man in buckskins, employing vastly different tones. "Once again you have fully justified my confidence in your ability to cope in the best possible way with a situation of some delicacy and danger."

"I'm not sorry it's over," the smaller figure went on, also

changing "his" manner of speaking. "This beard you gave me itches, Manny."

"And doesn't do a thing to improve your beauty, light of my life," the first supporter declared.

Even at such close quarters, so effective had been the changes they had wrought to their appearances, it was not until they reverted to their normal voices that Ole Devil realized he was speaking to Corrinne and Mangrove Hallistead.

Amused by the expression of amazement on the young Texian's normally emotionless face, the entertainer made an explanation. He had assumed the disguise as an aid to tracking down a spy in Santa Anna's pay on the day that Ole Devil had left San Felipe. Having achieved his purpose early that afternoon, he had been about to bathe, shave, and put on his usual clothes when he had heard that the withdrawal was to be resumed. Guessing that there would be protests against the decision, he had suggested that his wife don suitable attire so they could mingle with the enlisted men unnoticed and, if necessary, warn General Houston of what was happening.

Having joined the protest meeting and seen Mannen Blaze hurrying away, the Hallisteads had deduced his purpose. They had also guessed that Ole Devil would take some form of action to disperse it. As Houston had crossed the river to examine the situation, they had waited to find out how the young captain would set about the task and were ready to support him.

Being just as knowledgeable as Ole Devil about mob psychology, Hallistead had known how he could best render aid. It was unlikely that any member of the crowd would want to take the lead if it appeared some other person was willing to assume the responsibility. So he had become the "agitator," then moved to another position to act as the "supporter." His comments on emerging had turned the gathering's feelings against the "agitator," who they assumed had lacked the courage of his convictions when challenged. Fortunately, possibly because of the tension his actions had evoked, nobody who had stood near Hallistead when he was playing the "agitator" was perceptive enough to have noticed the change in his behavior when he had turned to being the "supporter."

"I thought they'd be willing to change their minds about marching south when they saw there was more than just Manny against it," Corrinne continued, her feminine tones at odds with her masculine appearance. "And they did."

"You timed your entrance to perfection, as always, light of my life," the entertainer agreed. "But General Houston will have to engage the enemy soon, or the advantage we have gained for him will be dissipated."

"He'll be doing it before long," Ole Devil guessed. "And when he does, we'll settle who's going to control Texas once and for all."

The young Texian's words were prophetic!

16
ME NO ALAMO, ME NO GOLIAD

Major General Samuel Houston's insistence upon waiting until the time and the place were right before allowing the confrontation with *Presidente* Antonio Lopez de Santa Anna's column was fully justified by the events of Thursday, April 21, 1836.

Bringing about such a desirable state of affairs had not been easy. In spite of the way in which the protest meeting at Groce's Place had been dispersed by Ole Devil Hardin and the Hallisteads, there had been considerable discontentment among the enlisted men as the march continued with no suggestion of what its ultimate purpose might be. Wanting to avoid disappointment and a complete breakdown of morale if his judgment of the situation should prove at fault, the general did not offer to enlighten them. As he was to say in later years, "I consulted none, nor held no councils of war. If I was to err, the blame would be mine alone."

Notwithstanding Houston's reticence, some of the more astute men under his command began to realize that something was developing. While their dependants were continuing to move eastward under a small escort, the route being taken by the rest of the army was to the southeast.

Then, on April 18—when spirits were approaching their lowest ebb and badly needed a boost—came astounding news that supplied it. No longer was the Republic of Texas's Army withdrawing ahead of their pursuers. Now the position was reversed, and it was the Mexicans who were in front.

For the first time Houston made a pronouncement to his men. Telling them something of the geography in that part of Texas, he had stated that Santa Anna was close to San Jacinto Bay. The only way *el Presidente* could rejoin the main body of his army was by crossing at Lynch's Ferry, or by the bridge that spanned Vince's Bayou. By increasing their pace, the Texians could reach whichever point was selected ahead of their enemies.

"Victory is certain!" the general cried. "Trust in God and fear not! And remember the Alamo! Above all, remember the Alamo!"

"Remember the Alamo!" came the answering reply, as if in one voice and with a vehemence that boded little good for those who had been responsible for its fall.

El Presidente's fury-inspired headlong dash for Harrisburg had proved a waste of time. On his arrival he found that the town was practically deserted. Forewarned of his coming, President Burnet, the government, their escort of New Orleans Wildcats, and almost all of the population had taken a hurried departure. From three captives he had learned that the objects of his hatred were fleeing to Galveston with the intention of leaving the country by boat.

Dispatching Colonel Juan Almonte with a force of cavalry to check on Lynch's Ferry and New Washington, both at the mouth of the San Jacinto River, Santa Anna had allowed the rest of his exhausted force some badly needed rest. Then, according to a report he received, there was a chance to end the rebellion with a single stroke. Apparently making for safety east of the Trinity River, Houston and his men were going toward Lynch's Ferry. Thwarted of his vengeance in one direction, *el Presidente* swore to take it in another.

Starting the march once more, Santa Anna drove his men even harder. In his excitement and eagerness he completely overlooked the fact that the terrain he was entering offered only a limited opportunity for maneuvering so large a force. To the left was Buffalo Bayou, ahead the estuary of the San Jacinto River, at the right the inlets and swamps of Galveston Bay, and, after the crossing of the bridge over Vince's Bayou, they had water to the rear as well.

On the face of it *el Presidente* had nothing to fear. Not only was General Ramirez Sesma at Thompson's Ferry with a thousand men and General Vincente Filisola close by at the head of another eighteen hundred, but his own force was more than double that led by Houston. So it mattered not that General Antonio Gaona was lost somewhere with two battalions or that General José Urrea had sent word that he was returning with his brigade to put down an Indian uprising in the state of Tamaulipa.[1] He had no need of any of them, nor any desire to allow them a share in the glory of driving the "foreign land thieves" from his domain.

So things stood when, on the twentieth of April, the two forces came face-to-face close to the confluence of Buffalo Bayou and the San Jacinto River. There was some sporadic and indecisive fighting during the day, with Houston wisely restraining his men's eagerness to get to close quarters. Not only had the size of his command been decreased by the escort for their dependants, there was a larger loss. Apart from Company C, whose commanding officer he regarded as a good-luck talisman, he had sent the Texas Light Cavalry to make a feint in the direction of Thompson's Ferry.

Annoyed by the refusal of the enemy to play into his hands, Santa Anna had pulled back to make camp for the night. He was most satisfied by the site he selected. It was on a hill, well protected against flanking attacks by having water to the rear, thick woodland to the right as far as the banks of the San Jacinto River, and open terrain to the left, with a clear front between it and the Texians. Furthermore, late in the afternoon, General Martin Perfecto de Cós had arrived with four hundred men and one of *el Presidente*'s baggage wagons carrying pow-

1. As is explained in *Get Urrea,* there was a far more sinister reason for the departure of the Tamaulipa Brigade.—J.T.E.

der and shot to replace that which had been expended or ruined in the dash across country.

Gathering his officers in the evening, General Houston outlined his strategy. "Deaf" Smith and his scouts were to go and destroy Vince's bridge, cutting off the enemies' retreat and preventing, or at least delaying, the arrival of further reinforcements. Everybody else was to make preparations for an all-out assault upon *el Presidente*'s camp the following morning. In conjunction with the latter, there had been something that demanded attention. Sent by Colonel Edward Fog to keep an eye on Cós's party, a patrol from the Texas Light Cavalry had captured a Mexican deserter, who informed them of what the baggage wagon was transporting. On hearing about it, Houston had seen how he might be able to turn it to his ends.

Space does not permit a detailed account of how Ole Devil and Tommy Okasi, who became an "Indian" again for the mission, infiltrated Santa Anna's encampment in the night with the intention of destroying the newly arrived supply of ammunition. Suffice to say that they succeeded in concealing among the cargo an explosive device, equipped with a simple delayed-action detonator produced by a gunsmith in Houston's force. It was set to go off approximately when it would be needed the next day, complete accuracy being unattainable.

As if in repayment for his unflinching adherence to the correct policy over the past weeks and as a recompense for the misfortunes that had recently befallen the Texians' cause, the weather on the twenty-first of April was ideally suited for Houston's purpose. Not only had the night and dawn been wet and damp, there was a heavy fog, which made it possible for he and his seven hundred and eighty-three men to approach their enemy over open ground without being seen from a distance.

Carrying out the prediction made by Mangrove Hallistead at Groce's Place, Houston was in the lead. Sword in hand, as the fog began to lift, he waited for the most effective moment. Spread out in a thin, long line, his men were grasping their weapons eagerly. In addition to those equipped from the consignment, so many of the remainder had already owned caplocks that there were few weapons fired by flint and priming powder.

All was set for the attack!

With a shattering roar, touched off by the device that Ole Devil and Tommy had planted, the powder in the wagon at the center of the Mexicans' camp exploded.

Instantly Houston gave the order to charge!

There were no massed bands to urge the Texians on with the stirring notes of the "Degüello." All they could muster by way of music was a single fife and drum, whose players knew but one tune. So the attack went under way to the strains of *"Will You Come to the Bower I Have Shaded for You?"*

Nor was any further inducement necessary.

Taken by surprise, the Mexicans were at a further disadvantage. All but a favored few held antiquated weapons, in the use of which they had received little training. What was more, being flintlocks, the arms possessed a deadly failing in such inclement weather. Striking wet frizzen pans, what few sparks were produced by the flints fell onto damp and ruined priming powder.

Such an affliction did not affect the Texians. Their weapons were unimpaired by the elements. Just how many of the foe they killed with the devastating volley that they poured into the camp on Houston's command will never be known, but the figure must have been high. Following upon it, the Texians dashed furiously into their enemies' midst to continue the work with bayonets, swords, pistols, knives, or the butts of rifles.

Already exhausted and dispirited by the hardships inflicted upon them during the forced march, demoralized by the discovery that their weapons refused to function when those of their assailants dealt out death and destruction, the Mexicans essayed only a minimal token resistance.

Many sought to save their lives in flight.[2] Ramón Caro was

2. Colonel Juan Almonte fled from the field of battle unscathed, but on discovering that all avenues of escape were blocked, returned after the fighting was over to surrender "with honor."—J.T.E.

one of their number, but he was captured by "Deaf" Smith's scouts on his way south.

Others—and they were plentiful—hoping to gain mercy by disassociating themselves from certain events that had been calculated to arouse the Texians' ire, flung down their weapons and yelled in broken English, "Me no Alamo, me no Goliad!"

Not all the pleas were successful. It would be futile to suggest that all who wished were allowed to surrender. A few were cut down with their arms raised, but not as many as might have been the case if the positions had been reversed.

There were those, too, who fought as best they could. Among them was General Manuel Fernandez Castrillón, who fell after refusing a suggestion that he should flee on the grounds that, "I've never shown my back to an enemy and I'm too old to do it now."

In not more than eighteen minutes from the explosion, for which at least the young Mexican officer who had been involved in the killing of James Bowie at the Alamo Mission had cause to be grateful,[3] the Battle of San Jacinto was over.

Six hundred and thirty Mexicans lay dead and a further seven hundred, a figure that increased as strays were gathered in, were taken prisoner.

The cost to the Texians?

Nine dead, only two of whom were killed by bullets, and twenty-three wounded!

And what of the person who was responsible for the terrible loss of life?

There was not a trace to be found of *Presidente* Antonio Lopez de Santa Anna on the field at San Jacinto.

Perhaps it is only fitting, considering the part Ole Devil Hardin had already played in bringing about *el Presidente*'s downfall, that the following occurred.

While leading a patrol that was helping to round up the scattered Mexican soldiers on the day after the battle, the young Texian came upon a forlorn and ignoble figure hiding among a clump of bushes. Although he was clad in the cheap

3. For details, read *Get Urrea* and *The Quest for Bowie's Blade*.—J.T.E.

and tattered garments of an *Activos* enlisted man, having discarded his fine raiment before fleeing on seeing that the tide of battle was going against him, Ole Devil recognized the self-styled "Napoleon of the West." If further proof had been needed, it was supplied by the Mexican prisoners' shouts of *"El Presidente! El Presidente!"* as the captive was being escorted through their ranks on the way to General Houston's headquarters.

With the Battle of San Jacinto fought and won, the way was open for Texas to become a part of the United States. It did not come in a short while, nor easily, but—as he had done all through the struggle to win independence, Jackson Baines Hardin continued to play his part in the developments and to uphold his reputation as being a "lil ole devil for a fight."

APPENDIX A

Although Jackson Baines "Ole Devil" Hardin had been proven innocent of the murder that had caused him to flee Louisiana, the reasons outlined in *Ole Devil and the Caplocks* prevented him from returning. So, having accepted Texas as his permanent home, he had thrown himself wholeheartedly into the struggle for independence. Given the rank of captain and placed in command of Company C, Texas Light Cavalry—a regiment raised and equipped by the Hardin, Fog, and Blaze clan—he had shown himself to be a very capable fighting officer. Not only had he an inborn flair for leadership, he was capable of enforcing his wishes by physical means when necessary. He was helped in this by having a thorough knowledge of *savate*, French foot and fist boxing, augmented with several jujitsu and karate tricks learned from Tommy Okasi.[1] In addition, he was superbly armed and expert in the use of weapons.

Made by the Arkansas master blacksmith and cutler, James

1. Ole Devil Hardin never attained the skill of another member of the clan to whom Tommy Okasi imparted the secrets of jujitsu and karate. This was Captain Dustine Edward Marsden "Dusty" Fog, C.S.A., details of whose career are given in the author's "Floating Outfit" and "Civil War" series.

Black, who produced the original for James Bowie,[2] Ole Devil's knife was a copy of that famous weapon. Sixteen inches in overall length, weighing forty-three ounces, it had a lugged brass hilt, a concave ivory handle, and a scolloped brass butt cap. Its eleven-inch-long blade was two and a quarter inches wide and three eights of an inch thick at the stock. Only the last five and a quarter inches of the back of the blade was sharpened. This made a concave arc to join the main cutting surface and form a "clip" point.[3]

Although the knife, Ole Devil's matched brace of percussion-fired, British-made Manton .54-caliber single-shot pistols and Haiman Bros. saber were conventional arms, the same could not be said of his rifle. It was in fact a successful attempt by the Mormon gunsmith Jonathan Browning,[4] to produce a weapon capable of firing several shots in succession without the need to reload in the usual manner after each one.

Fifty-eight and seven eighths inches in length, the octagonal barrel accounting for forty and five sixteenths of an inch of this, the Browning Slide Repeating rifle weighed nine pounds fourteen ounces. The "Slide," a rectangular iron bar with holes to accommodate the powder, shot, and percussion caps—generally five in number, as this was the size that could be carried most conveniently, but longer slides could be had as a special order—was placed through an aperture in the rifle's breech. A thumb-operated lever on the right side of the frame caused the slide to advance until each chamber moved into line with the barrel's bore, then cammed it forward to obtain a gas-tight seal.

Ole Devil's "granddaughter," Betty Hardin, also acquired considerable ability in both these martial arts.—J.T.E.

2. Some researchers claim that James Bowie's oldest brother, Rezin Pleasant, was the actual designer of the knife.—J.T.E.

3. The dimensions have been duplicated by master cutler William D. "Bo" Randall, Jr., of Orlando, Florida, in his Model 12 "Smithsonian" bowie knife, one of which is carried by James Allenvale "Bunduki" Gunn, see *Bunduki, Bunduki and Dawn* and *Sacrifice for the Quagga God* by J.T.E.

4. Jonathan Browning's eldest son, John Moses (1855–1926), became the world's most prolific and, arguably, finest designer of firearms. He makes a "guest appearance" in *Calamity Spells Trouble*.—J.T.E.

The hammer was underneath the frame, in front of the trig-
gerguard, within easy reach of the forefinger, so the piece could
be cocked without removing it from the shoulder.

In spite of the difficulty of transporting the rifle with the slide
in position, it was simple in design and operation, as well as
being capable of continuous fire far in excess of any contemporary weapon. However, during the period when he was manufacturing it, between 1834 and 1842, he lacked the facilities to
go into large-scale production. He would have been able to do
so in later years, but the development of self-contained metallic
cartridges and more compact, if less simple, repeating arms
made it obsolete.[5]

5. While engaged in manufacturing the Slide Repeating rifle, Jonathan
Browning also developed a rifle that could be discharged six times in succession. The ammunition was held in a cylinder similar to that of later
revolvers, but there was no mechanism, and it had to be rotated manually
after each shot. While the same caliber—approximately .45—and almost
ten inches shorter, it was more bulky and weighed twelve pounds two
ounces. It was not offered for sale until he had settled in Council Bluffs,
Utah, in 1852. By that time, due to the ever-increasing availability of Samuel Colt's mechanically superior rifles and revolvers, it, too, had become
redundant.—J.T.E.

APPENDIX B

The author regrets that he is unable to say why Tommy Okasi, a trained *samurai*,[1] should have been compelled to leave Japan with no possibility of ever returning.[2] Even his true name cannot be divulged. The one he used was an Americanized corruption of that which he had given when taken, as the sole survi-

1. samurai: A member of the Japanese lower nobility's elite warrior class, who usually served as a retainer for the *daimyos,* the hereditary feudal barons. A masterless samurai who became a mercenary was known as a *ronin.* From the mid-1800s, increased contact with the Western Hemisphere brought an ever-growing realization that the retention of a hereditary and privileged warrior class was not compatible with the formation of a modern and industrialized society. Various edicts issued by the emperor between 1873 and 1876 abolished the special rights of the samurai, and although some of their traditions, concepts, and military skills were retained, they ceased to exist in their original form.—J.T.E.
2. The various members of the Hardin, Fog, and Blaze clan with whom I discussed the subject while visiting Fort Worth, Texas, in 1975 said that, because of the circumstances and the high social standing of the people involved—all of whom have descendants holding positions of influence and importance in Japan at the time of writing—it is inadvisable even at this late date to make public the facts concerning the reason for Tommy Okasi's departure.—J.T.E.

vor, from a derelict vessel in the China Sea by a ship under the command of Ole Devil Hardin's father. His only possessions were a *daisho* of matched swords[3]—comprising of a *tachi* with a thirty-inch-long blade and a *wakizashi* about half of the former's length—made of an exceptionally high-quality steel,[4] a six-foot-long bow of a style peculiar to his nation,[5] and a selection of different kinds of arrows.[6]

3. Traditionally, the *daisho* was carried thrust into the sash about the samurai's waist, in which case the longer sword was called a *katana*. As Tommy Okasi spent a considerable amount of his time on horseback after he arrived in the United States, he found it more convenient to wear his suspended by their sheaths on either side of a leather belt.—J.T.E.
4. After the blade had been shaped by fusing together numerous layers of steel, it was ready to be tempered. A claylike material, for which every master swordsmith had his own secret recipe, was applied to the whole of the blade apart from an inch or so at the tip and along the entire cutting edge. After heating the blade to the correct temperature—which by tradition was commenced in the half-light of the early morning—it was plunged into a tub of cold water. The exposed metal cooled instantly and became very hard. Being encased in the clay sheath, the rest of the metal lost its heat more gradually and, remaining comparatively soft, was given a greater pliancy. To prove that the finished product was capable of carrying out the work for which it was intended, the smith beat it against a sheet of iron and hacked to pieces the body of a dead criminal before handing it over to the owner. This is of course only a simplified description of the process.—J.T.E.
5. Unlike Occidental "self" bows of the period, with the stave formed from a single billet of timber, the Japanese weapon was built of three bamboo strips sheathed on two sides with mulberry wood. This formed a core, which was encased by further lengths of bamboo, the whole pasted together with fish glue and painted with laquer. By laminating the bamboo and the softer, more pliable, mulberry wood, a great strength and flexibility were achieved.

How Tommy Okasi strung his bow is described in *Ole Devil and the Mule Train,* and a comparison with one Occidental method when using a modern recurved—where the ends of the limbs are bent back from the straight line—composite hunting bow (with some form of fiberglass limbs and a wooden handle riser), can be made by reading *Sacrifice for the Quagga God*—J.T.E.
6. The traditional Japanese arrow was made from *mashino-dake,* a very hard, straight, and thin species of bamboo. After being cut in the winter, the bamboo was left to dry outdoors until spring. After it had been further

In addition to being an expert with the weapons and a reasonable shot with a pistol or rifle, the latter skill having been acquired after his arrival in the United States,[7] he was also a master of jujitsu and karate. As these forms of unarmed combat were practically unheard of in the Western Hemisphere at that time,[8] they were useful in helping to offset any disadvantages in height and weight when he found himself in conflict with larger or heavier men.

---

dried and hardened by being placed close to a fire, the joints were carefully smoothed down. When the shaft had been polished with emery powder and water, it was once more exposed to the fire. Finally it was fletched with three feathers from a hawk, falcon, or eagle and had its nock and some form of metal arrowhead affixed.

The *karimata*, "forked arrow" point—which Tommy Okasi did not find cause to use on the assignment described in this work—was a two-pronged design with extremely sharp cutting edges. Originally intended to sever ropes and leather armor lacings, it was also an extremely potent weapon. The width varied from one to six inches between the tips of the prongs. Because of the terrible injuries they were capable of inflicting, the larger sizes—none of which Tommy had in his possession—were also called "bowel rakers."

In conclusion the author feels that a brief description of the Japanese technique called *yabusame*—translated literally, "shooting from a running horse"—may be of interest. In competition, the mounted *kyudoka* rides at a gallop over a course two *cho*—roughly two hundred and thirty-eight yards—in length, along which are placed at approximately thirty-eight, one hundred and eighteen, and one hundred and ninety-three yards, two-foot-square wooden targets on posts between thirty-six and forty-eight inches high. Passing them at a distance of around thirty yards, the *kyudoka* discharges an arrow with a forked head that shatters on impact.—J.T.E.

7. Although early types of firearms had been known in Japan since the arrival of Portuguese explorers in 1543, the samurai had small regard for them as weapons and spent little time in learning how to use them.—J.T.E.

8. Until the visits by a flotilla under the command of Commodore Perry, United States Navy, in 1853–54 paved the way, there was little contact between Japan and the Western World.—J.T.E.